Frogmorton

Drawings by

ERNEST H. SHEPARD

SUSAN COLLING

Frogmorton

NEW YORK : ALFRED · A · KNOPF

This title was originally catalogued by the Library of Congress as follows:

Colling, Susan   Frogmorton; illus. by Ernest H. Shepard.
1. Animals-Stories   2. Christmas stories   I. Title
Library of Congress Catalog Card Number: 56-5719
ISBN: 0-394-81175-5, 0-394-91175-X (Lib. ed.)

TO

Amanda

WITH LOVE

Contents

Illustrations

Frogmorton

CHAPTER ONE

The Beginning

Frederick Fitzherbert Frog lived at Frogmorton Fall in Frobishire. He hunted and shot and fished, and did all the right things. He also smoked a pipe after dinner, put on his carpet slippers, and sat with his feet in the fender and enjoyed life.

His old friend Timothy Ptolemy Tortoise lived in a bed-sitting room at the back of a dirty block of flats in London. He spent five and a half days a week in a stuffy old office in the City, smoked very cheap cigarettes, and sometimes had a shilling on a horse which never seemed to come in first. He was very poor and he didn't enjoy life at all.

One day about the middle of December poor old Timothy Tortoise was shuffling down Piccadilly trying not to bump into too many people, or rather, trying to avoid too many people bumping

Sat with his feet in the fender and enjoyed life

into him—everyone seemed in such a hurry. Timothy Tortoise was never in a hurry because he just hadn't anything to be in a hurry about. Every time he was bumped into, he said, "I beg your pardon," or "Excuse me," or "My fault, I'm sure," and raised his hat, because he was really a very polite tortoise and had been beautifully brought up. And each time he did this, little flakes of snow slipped down inside the collar of his old mackintosh and sat with little icy bumps on the top of his bald head. It was very, very uncomfy.

Suddenly he tripped on the edge of the curbstone and, looking up, he saw a familiar figure riding by, seated right on top of a No. 14 bus.

He didn't enjoy life at all

"Bless my soul," he exclaimed, "it's Father Christmas."

And then all the hurry and the bustle suddenly had a meaning—Christmas! How could he have been so stupid! The lights in the shop windows. The tinsel and the colored glass bobbles. The holly at the street corners. All the bright paper parcels the people were carrying. Timothy, who was used to shuffling along with his nose pointing in the gutter, suddenly looked up and sniffed the air. Why! even the air smelled of Christmas! It was sharp, exciting, challenging. "Parcels tied with colored string," thought Timothy. "A Christmas tree with candles on and children dancing round and me dancing too, playing 'Blind Man's Buff' and 'Kiss in the Ring.' "

The memory of it all was so sharp, he could almost taste the smell of crackers being pulled and burned-out candles and orange jelly. And then he thought, "What a fool I am! What a silly old fool, standing here in the street, dreaming of those far-away days. No crackers for me or a parcel tied with colored string. I shouldn't think that Father Christmas even knows that I'm still alive." And a great big lump came up in his throat before he could stop it, and a tear the size of a pickled onion splashed onto the top of his galoshes.

"Stupid old fool," he muttered to himself, now
very cross and put out. He slipper-sloppered along

Seated right on top of a No. 14 *bus*

the edge of the pavement as fast as he could, trying hard not to be knocked over by the crowd or a passing taxi.

He had negotiated Fortnum and Mason's and was just passing a chemist's shop when he felt a tremendous blow in the back, and a gruff voice which was more like a croak said, "Timothy, my dear old boy, I thought you were dead. Great heavens! What a surprise meeting you! And in London of all places!"

Looking round and blinking, Timothy saw his old friend Frederick Frog. He wore a big thick overcoat, which must have belonged to his grandfather for it was rather old-fashioned, a curly bowler hat, tight pin-striped trousers, shiny black patent leather button boots with white spats, and he carried a beautifully rolled-up umbrella and a pair of pale primrose chamois leather gloves. Timothy thought he looked magnificent.

"Well!" he exclaimed in a startled little voice, and then, "Well, well," and gave a sort of a gulp and didn't know how to go on. This was his old, old friend of years ago, his good old friend Froggy, and here he was standing in the middle of London, looking at him. It seemed too good to be true.

Looking round, Timothy saw his old friend
Frederick Frog

"I was just going round to Noodles. Now we'll both go together," said Frog in a very matter-of-fact tone of voice, which was his normal sort of voice anyhow.

Poor Timothy looked down at his dirty old mackintosh and his pudgy old umbrella which would *not* roll up properly, however hard he tried, and said, "Oh, dear" (to himself), and then, "I'm very sorry Froggy, but I'm afraid I can't come. You

see, I'm no longer a member of Noodles. I had to
give up my subscription many years ago and I
haven't been near the place since."

"Nonsense, my dear fellow," said Frog, "you
come along with me. We'll have a drink together
and I'll make you a member all over again, you
see if I don't." And taking Timothy's arm, he pro-
pelled him forcibly down Piccadilly and round
the corner of St. James's Street and right up the
steps and straight into the bar of Noodles Club
almost before poor Timothy Tortoise could get his
breath.

It was all very unreal and flabbergasting. Timothy accepted a glass of sherry and then another
one, and began to feel a warm comforting glow
creeping up very slowly from his toes to his chin
—or at the place where his chin would have been
if he'd had one.

"Where are you going for Christmas, old man?"
asked Frog in the same happy, jolly matter-of-fact
voice, as though going away for Christmas was the
most normal and everyday thing in the world.

"Er—er—well-l," began Timothy, but before he
could get any further Frog butted in:

"Staying at home, eh? Can't stay at 'ome for
Christmas. Come down to Frogmorton and spend

it with me. I'm on me own. Me nephews and nieces all grown up—no relations left. All dead. What d'you say?"

"Oh," stammered Timothy. "Oh, my goodness, Froggy my dear old friend! Well, well! That *would* be lovely. I really *should* enjoy that. D'you know I don't suppose I've been away to stay with anyone for thirty years! Are you sure it wouldn't be a bother to you?"

"Bother? Bother? You a bother? Of course not. I'll soon tell you if you are. And furthermore, you must stay as long as you like. Any good at gardening?"

"Of, yes," said Timmy, "I used to be quite a good gardener, but I don't think I've been in a proper garden for years and years and years." And all of a sudden he felt the crumbly earth behind his nails and the smell of damp leaves and chrysanthemums sharp in his nostrils and his heart gave a little leap of delight.

" 'Course there's nothing much to be done at present with all this frost and snow about but, fact is, I've had to let three of the gardeners go. Can't afford to keep 'em these days. Now there's only old Grubbins and a half-witted boy left. Have to help 'em meself sometimes. Can't say I like it. Don't

know one plant from another, so you'll be a great
help to me, Timmy, old boy. When can you come,
by the way? What about next Tuesday? Always
think Tuesday's a good day for travellin'. Have to
come in to Coppertown on Tuesday, anyhow, so I
could pick you up."

"Oh, yes, Tuesday would suit splendidly," said
Timothy quickly, afraid that something would
happen in the meantime to stop this glorious
dream from turning into reality. After all, there
were only five days until Tuesday. Five days would
pass somehow or other and surely nothing would
happen in that time to prevent him taking this
wonderful opportunity to get out into the country
and breathe healthy, strong, country air again. Oh!
it was a splendid idea! And he was the luckiest tortoise in the whole of England!

(Here I must explain that Timmy was unlike
other tortoises in that he did not sleep all through
the winter. He suffered from insomnia. Which
means that he was an habitually bad sleeper, poor
old fellow. And when other tortoises were safely
snuggled away in their beds till springtime, he
shuffled about the London streets, feeling cold and
miserable).

"Dear Froggy," he said, "how can I thank you

enough? You don't know what this means to me. You just don't." And because of the heat of the room and the firelight after the cold outside and perhaps because of the two glasses of sherry, which he was quite unaccustomed to, poor Timothy Tortoise suddenly melted like a chocolate blanc-

The tears ran down his face in rivers

mange. The tears ran down his face in rivers, and
made a great lake on the crimson carpet. In fact,
he had to be mopped up by Frog and the bar-
man (whose name was Proudfoot) with sponges and
tea cloths, and wrapped up in old copies of the
Financial Times, and placed in front of the fire to
dry.

"There now," said Frog at last, who was rather
embarrassed by any sign of emotion at any time,
let alone a veritable flood like this one. "Don't
worry any more about anything. Tuesday it is. I've
written it all down for you on this piece of paper.
Don't lose it. You catch the one-thirty train from
Paddington Station, change at Slithering Junction
and arrive at Coppertown at 4.20 p.m. That is, if
the train is punctual, which it never is. I will meet
you there and all being well, we will get home in
time for tea. Now, if you're sure you're all right I
must leave you an' go and attend to a little private
business that needs clearin' up." And with that and
a final friendly pat on the back, though not such
a hard one this time, he was gone.

Timothy sat staring into the fire for fully five minutes after he had gone, still so overcome with emotion that he could hardly trust himself to stand up.
Christmas with Froggy! Christmas in the country!

A garden! A great big garden with a greenhouse or possibly two greenhouses. Apples and nuts and probably a decanter of port! Oh! the glorious vision of it all! It was too much—really *too* much!

He put his hand in his pocket (the only pocket which hadn't a hole in it) and pulled out a bus ticket, two pennies, a sixpence, and a half-crown. With as much dignity as he could muster, he handed the sixpence to Proudfoot, retrieved his ancient mackintosh and his battered umbrella, and clutching the half-crown in one rather sticky paw, tottered out of the Club and into the pale winter afternoon light.

It had finished snowing and the sun peeped over the edge of a big black cloud. The half-crown had been meant for two large ham sandwiches and a glass of beer. That didn't matter now. What did anything matter? He must go and buy a Christmas present for his old friend Froggy.

CHAPTER TWO

Frogmorton Hall

THE TRAIN arrived twenty minutes late at Coppertown station. It really couldn't help it. It was a little old train which had been huffing and puffing away for a great many years. The single track line up which it puffed the eleven miles to Coppertown from Slithering Junction wound round corners and through woods and under tunnels and always up, up, up, till sometimes the poor old thing felt its rusty, aching joints would fall apart and its ancient heart of iron would burst. But it never did.

When it reached the top of Gallowtree Hill, the grave little engine hooted for joy three times and plunged recklessly down the remaining bit of the journey as fast as its ricketty old wheels could go, singing, "Nearly there, nearly there, nearly there," all the way down into Coppertown. It arrived hot

Here is a picture of the train nearly arriving at the station

and panting and gasping for breath and—oh! so
pleased with itself, only to be pushed onto a sort of
turntable arrangement and made to turn round.
Then it was all back to front and contrary-wise, and
had to push itself all the way back again the way it
had come, which makes me think that the world is
very unkind to little old engines.

Timothy Tortoise had one remaining precious
possession and this was a watch left to him by his
great Uncle Ptolemy, a gold half-hunter watch which
really told the time and also had his initial on the
top in beautiful curly letters like that (only
better). So when it got to four o'clock and
then after four, each minute seemed like an hour and
he had to shake it up and down several times to see
it hadn't stopped.

After that, he leaned his head out of the carriage window, trying to get a first glimpse of
Coppertown, but he only got a smut in his eye
so he had to put it back again. Over the page
is a picture of the train nearly arriving at the station. You can't see Timmy of course, but *there* is
Frederick Frog starting up the car and there is old
Farmer Crossbones and his dog Shooter going to
meet Mrs. Crossbones off the train.

Frog's car was a 1922 model Rolls Royce. It still

went like a bird when wound up, but it took a bit of getting started. However, Frog managed to do it this time, after about ten minutes, which warmed him up while he waited for the train. You see, you never could tell, if by some freakish chance (it had happened once in 1912) the thing might be punctual, and then you would be late and that would never do. Frog was never late for anything.

Timmy helped to tie the battered old suitcase on the back and clambered inside with his little Gladstone bag clutched firmly in one paw.

"This all the luggage you've got?" asked Frog, who wasn't renowned for being tactful. "Where are yer hunting-boots and yer guns?"

Timothy didn't like to tell him that his hunting-boots and guns had been sold over twenty years ago, so he just stammered that he'd forgotten to bring them and then blushed to the tips of his ears. He wasn't used to telling lies and it *was* rather a whopper.

"Oh, never mind, never mind," said Frog. "We'll soon fix you up. I've got an old pair of Sturdy's I could lend you and as for huntin'—well, I'm ashamed to say, I haven't been out more than three times meself this season. Huntin' isn't what it used to be, yer know. All this wire about everywhere and that bloomin' fellah Goad throwing his weight about and unsettlin' everybody. Bill Badger's threatened to give in his notice *and* I don't blame 'im. Goad's a perfect menace, ought to be kicked out of the country."

Frog's slow anger was mounting in him, as it always did when he thought of Samuel Goad, the Mountebank, and instead of putting his foot on the accelerator, he suddenly stamped it down with all his force on the brake and they stopped with a sickening jerk, both noses jammed hard against the windshield.

"Sorry, old boy. Didn't mean to do that. Now I've gone and stalled the engine. Here, give us the handle." So saying, he jumped out and gave the handle a swing and it started up again at the third attempt. "Wonderful car!" said Frog. "Wouldn't change 'im for all the tea in China! Now we're off! Home in time for tea—I hope," he added under his breath.

All this time Timothy had been sitting staring round him—enrapt, entranced, and speechless with wonder. His hands and feet were numb with the cold in spite of the big fur rug Frog had wrapped cosily round him, and his nose belonged to him no longer and was just something to be remembered, but Timmy hardly noticed how cold he was. He just sat murmuring happily, "Oh! My goodness! Oh, just look! It's like a real Christmas card!"

And so it was. The old red sun was sinking down over the rim of the snow-covered hills. Half of him was still left and threw a pearly-pink glow over the world making it glimmer with flames, golden and pink and red like the inside of an opal. Below them was a light mist, a soft grey veil tinged with red, hanging over the valley, where the lights of Coppertown began to prick out in the twilight like sudden stars.

It was England and the country at Christmas time. Hints of things half-forgotten—the smell of wood smoke and the crackle of frozen leaves beneath your feet, the sharp bell-ringing "clack-clack" of an old cock pheasant as he flies home to roost—all these things suddenly became reality again to Timmy and he tingled all over with the touchable joy of it all.

"I'd forgotten," he murmured, "I'd really forgotten how perfectly beautiful it all was."

"What was that?" asked Frog. "Speak up, old man, I'm getting a bit deaf in me left ear. 'Beautiful,' you said? 'Course it's beautiful. Always was. Always will be, in spite of all the things they try to do to it. Here! See those trees over there? There's the avenue up to the house—beech trees—finest avenue

of beeches in the whole of Frobishire—planted by my
great-great-great-grandfather. Look! There's the
Lodge. Hope old Mrs. Woodcock's about, otherwise
I'll have to open the gates—or you will. Oh, no.
There she is. Must have seen the lights of the car.
Evenin', Mrs. Woodcock. How's Woodcock? Still in
bed with rheumatics? You must get 'im up, you
know. Won't do, lyin' in bed! Bed's no place to be
at Christmas! Tell 'im I said so."

And so they trundled on, Frog keeping up an endless monologue full of "tenants" and "rates" and
"taxes" and "holidays with pay," and so on and so
on, until they suddenly turned a sharp corner and
came into full view of the house standing at the far
end of its own magnificent avenue of beech trees. A
square Georgian house with pillars and colonnades
and a great double staircase of stone leading up to
the front door. Two lights only were visible from the
long windows, but the door was open and a flood
of light beckoned from the hall.

"Here we are! Home at last!" said Froggy. "Welcome to Frogmorton, Timmy old boy; home of the
Fitzherbert Frogs! Unvarnished, unpainted, half-
shut up and taxed almost out of existence, but still
standing, dear old boy, still standing. Come along
in and have a drink." And he half-pushed, half-

"Here we are! Home at last!" said Froggy.

dragged poor old Timothy up the steps and through
the enormous hall, which Timmy found very cold
and draughty and smelling of damp, into a little
tiny room at the end of a passage which Frog used
as his sitting-room, office, dining-room, and everything else except bedroom. (He insisted on going
upstairs to bed.)

After the cold, dimly-lit passages outside, the
sudden rush of warm air as they opened the door
was almost overpowering. It was a comfy, cosy,
higgledy-piggledy kind of room. Books and old
sporting prints lined the walls. Old fishing-rods and
baskets stood in corners. Guns, neatly stored in a
glass-fronted cupboard, glinted in the light of an
enormous log fire in front of which lay a funny old
floppity spaniel whose name was Matt, chiefly because he looked like one. He sat up and greeted
Frog with a smile and a wag of his tail, which was
a bit too long and looked like a pump handle.

"Good boy, good boy," said Frog. "Down, Matt.
Down." And Matt lay down again with his ears
over his eyes and went on dreaming. "Funny old
dog. Thinks 'e owns me, yer know. Expect 'e does
really. What are you having to drink—whisky,
sherry or Madeira?"

Timmy wanted all three but felt it would be more

polite to say, "Whatever you're having, Froggy."
So the two animals stood toasting their tails by the
fire and drank one another's health in a lovely deep
golden wine which had brought imprisoned sunshine all the way from the shores of Madeira.

They drank one another's health

A glorious warm, tired feeling crept up through
Timmy's old bones and he could only murmur,
"Well! Oh my!" and "So this is your home, Froggy?

Well, well, well!" The Fulham Road and his own
cold, dingy, stuffy little room (it was always cold
and stuffy somehow at the same time) seemed so
very far away, almost in another world.

"Yes," answered Frog gruffly, "this is my home."
And then, "That is until the tax collectors take it
from me." And he grunted and kicked at a falling
log with his foot. "But never mind all that now," he
added. "Drink up, my boy.

"Here's to to-day and here's to to-morrow.
  Here's to the way we can deal with our sorrow.
  Here's to brave hearts and here's to brave men.
  And here's to old England again and again.
  Never say 'Die' and never say 'Done.'
  Here's to my fishing-rod, here's to your gun.
  Here's to the hunting and here's to the fun.
  Here's to the battles still to be won——
  (I've forgotten how it goes on, but anyway),
  Here's to the two of us, both of us together,
  You and I, each one of us—er—er"

". . . and never mind the weather," he added
after a long pause. "That bit doesn't seem to fit in,
quite, does it?"

"Oh, I think it goes in all right," said Timothy.

"Did you make it up? All of it, I mean? The bit about England and everything?"

"Well, as a matter of fact, I did," said Frog, rather proud and embarrassed. "How on earth did you guess? Not exactly Shakespeare, yer know, but then I don't confess to be much of a poet."

"I think it's simply splendid," said Timmy. "Simply splendid," he repeated. "Splendiferous, in fact," he went on warming to the subject. "I wish I could write poetry."

"You will, old chap, you will," said Frog, giving him a friendly pat on the shoulder. "And now let's go into the kitchen and see what we're going to have for dinner."

"Oh, yes! Let's!" said Timmy, and arm in arm they walked happily down the passage, Frog humming a little tune to himself that he'd made up that morning and Timothy just musing in a lovely sort of comfy, musey way. Yes, it was going to be the happiest Christmas he had ever, ever had.

CHAPTER THREE

The Party

THE EARLY morning sun peeped through the curtains and said, "Good morning!" Timothy, who was still blissfully unconscious, blinked a sleepy eye at him, said "Morning" in a gruff sort of dreamy voice, and went on snoring for another hour until the door was opened quietly by Mrs. Grubbins, the gardener's wife, bringing him a cup of tea.

She was such a dear, quiet little person that he didn't really wake up until she was going out of the door and then it was too late to say "Thank you." Also, it took him more than a minute to realize where he was.

"Good gracious!" he muttered to himself as he stared round him and then he gave a sort of ecstatic little wriggle as he felt the delicious warmth of the soft feather bed and the lovely thin slippery linen sheets smelling of lavender, thickly embroidered on

She was such a dear, quiet little person

the hem with the Fitzherbert monogram. "Oh, my goodness! This is the life!" he thought to himself, as he bounced out of bed, looking at his watch and wondering if he'd be late for breakfast.

There had been another heavy fall of snow dur-

ing the night and the giant cedar tree outside the
far window was carrying a heavy white burden on
all its arms and seemed to be sighing with the
weight of it. But already the sun was melting some
of the white blanket on the roof and large pieces of
it were falling with great slithering thuds on to the
ground below.

"Hi, there!" called out Frog from somewhere underneath. "You awake yet? Breakfast's in and I'm
famished."

"Oh, yes, yes," shouted Timmy, not sure where he
ought to be shouting to, as he couldn't see Frog.
"I'm coming, I'm coming—but please don't wait for
me," he added hurriedly as he bundled himself into
his trousers and struggled manfully with his braces,
which somehow or other always managed to get
themselves into a tangle when he was in a hurry. (If
he ever was in a hurry, which was practically never,
as he had never had anything to be in a hurry
about.)

But, finally, they were anchored (though one of
them was on the wrong button), and his tie was
tied and his bootlaces done up, and the little piece
of fluff on the top of his cranium (head) was
brushed down (only to sit up again immediately in

The little piece of fluff was brushed down

the maddening way it always had), and he was ready.

As he opened the door, the most delicious smell of fried crackly bacon scented the air, the smell which of all smells is most heavenly to a hungry tortoise. He lifted up his nose, and sighed, "Oh, my; oh, my," and scuttled down the stairs as fast as his flappy old feet could carry him. For two pins he'd have slid down the banisters.

After breakfast, Frog, having lent Timmy a pair of stout wellington boots ("You can't walk about in those tissue paper things, my dear fellow"), took his friend round some of the garden. There were only a few places under the great big trees where they could walk, as all the rest of it was buried under two feet of snow.

"I'll have to ride into the village and get old Miss Hare to send the school children up to help clear some of this away," said Frog. "Bloomin' nuisance, it all is," he muttered. "Don't mind a covering of snow, does the garden good. . . . But all *this*," he said, pointing. "We never asked for all *this*."

Suddenly Timmy stopped in front of a small fir tree which stood apart from the others, as if in some way it had been singled out for a special purpose. Then he gulped and swallowed twice, and stammered: "Froggy—er—I say, Froggy——"

"Oh, come on, old man," said Frog rather impatiently. "What are you hangin' about for? What do you want with that old tree?"

"Well—er—er—well, what date is it to-day?" he blurted out suddenly.

"Wednesday," said Frog. "Why? What's that got to do with a tree?"

"Nothing—oh, n-n-nothing," stuttered Timmy. "I only just wondered that's all."

Froggy looked at him and then at the tree, and

back again at Timmy, shook his head, and muttered, "Blessed if I know what you're drivin' at," and was just going to move on when a little cock robin came and sat right on the topmost branch and shouted something quite rude at him in robin language and flew away.

"Bloomin' impertinence," muttered Frog. "Called me a stupid old woodenhead. Really, these robins are getting quite above themselves. I don't know what the world's comin' to."

And then as if in answer to an unspoken prayer that was whirling round deeply inside Timmy's mind and couldn't find its way out, a sudden flock of little birds arrived and each one of them perched itself on a different branch of the little fir tree. Frog blinked and looked again and saw that they were all different colored birds—blue tits, robins, and yellow-hammers—so that each one sitting at the end of a branch looked like a colored candle, and then the sun, shining through a piece of snow on the top, winked and made a perfect star.

"Good heavens," said Frog. "A Christmas tree! What a funny thing! And I'd forgotten all about one! So that was what you were trying to say, Timmy! It looks as if the birds have said it for you! It's Christmas Eve and we must have a Christmas tree! You and the birds seem to have decided which one it shall be, so I'll go and get a spade now and we'll dig it out and bring it in. What a silly old fool I am not to have thought of it before. After they've cleared the snow in front of the house, we'll have all the school children in and they can sing carols round it, and probably we'll have old Mrs. Moppett and the church choir too."

Frog was beginning to get quite excited at the idea and went hurriedly on. "Yes, yes, yes, of course! Christmas Eve! We always have the children in. I must tell Mrs. Grubbins to find some cake and biscuits and ginger wine. What a business it all is! Come on, Timmy. We must get busy!"

Timmy looked up at Frog and his face was beaming. "Oh, how lovely," he said. "May I decorate the Christmas tree, please, Froggy?"

"Of course, of course," said Frog, "if you can find anything to do it with. Come on now, don't stand about. There's work to be done." And with that he trotted off busily to fetch a spade. Timmy followed behind, a look of sublime happiness covering his face.

And so Christmas Eve finally became evening. The star that guided the Three Wise Men to Bethlehem shone out in the gathering twilight like a beacon light. So bright it was and so beautiful that suddenly, as if drawn by the nod of a single great conductor, all the little animals who had been working so busily clearing away the snow from Frog's front door, threw down their spades and shovels and raised their voices in a song which rose like a benediction in the frosty air.

Timmy, who was putting the finishing touches to the Christmas tree, heard it and joined in and Frog opened the front door and listened too. Then all the little animals trooped in, the rabbits, the squirrels, the hares, the hedgehogs, and one or two tiny field mice, singing as they went. The last to arrive was old Malvoleon, the mole, who had been busy making Christmas puddings on the lawn until somebody got word to him that there was a party at the Hall. Then he scuttled along as fast as his underground tunnels would take him and arrived in through a special entrance in the cellar, which nobody knew about except him.

Timmy had put a small bag of nuts, tied up in pink paper, on the Christmas tree for everybody including himself. There was a piece of plum cake and an apple for all the school children, and ginger wine and cups of steaming hot cocoa were handed round by Mr. and Mrs. Grubbins. Two enormous tree trunks burned on the great hall fire so that the animals could sit and toast their toes and roast chestnuts in the blaze.

It really was a lovely party and Frog, who usually found such functions rather timesome and looked forward to getting them over, was infected by Timmy's enthusiasm and thoroughly enjoyed himself. He cracked jokes with his tenants and tweaked the children's ears and made a bowl of hot rum-punch for the older members of the party. All the while old Timmy flipper-flappered backwards and forwards between one little group and another, organizing games of "Kiss in the ring" and "Blind Man's Buff" and "Apple Bobbin," until he didn't know whether he was coming or going and had to sit down in a corner to find out.

At last the last apple had been bobbed for, the last chestnut had popped out of the fire, and Timothy had handed out the last dregs from the punch bowl. All the little animals, happy and replete, began to put on their mufflers and woolly gloves and file past Frog to say, "Good-bye and thank you for the nice party," very politely and go home.

"Well, that's over," sighed Frog as he slumped

down in a big arm-chair and thrust out his toes to the dying fire.

"Yes," said Timmy sadly. "It's all over now. What a lovely party, Froggy. I hope they all enjoyed it as much as I did. It took me back to my childhood again."

"You needn't worry about that, old man," put in Frog quickly. "You've never left it. You're just a funny old baby still, aren't you?"

"Yes, I suppose I am. I s'pose I am," said Timothy. "I suppose I'll never grow up, will I?"

"You don't have to, old friend," said Frog, giving him an affectionate squeeze of the paw. "Like you better as you are. Too few nice people left in the world. You just stay as you are."

Then knocking out his pipe against the corner of the fireplace, he added: "Well, what do you say to a bit of bo-peep? Don't know about you, but I'm jolly sleepy. Shall we just go and look in the larder first?"

"Oh yes, let's," said Timothy quickly and then, as Frog turned to kick one of the dying embers of the fire back into the hearth, he suddenly grabbed his arm, and said in an urgent whisper, "Froggy, d'you —d'you—d'you think HE'LL come to-night?"

"Who'll come?" asked the unimaginative Frog.

"F-father Christmas," said Timothy, and blushed right over his ears. "I saw him, Froggy. Really, I did. He was in London doing some shopping. He must be frightfully busy. I don't suppose he'd have time to come down here, would he?"

"Oh, no," said Frog. "Anyway, he only comes to children." Then seeing the disappointed look in Timmy's eyes, he added, "Still you never know. Do you hang your stocking up when you're in London?"

"Oh, yes," replied Timmy, "I always do."

"Have you ever got anything in it?"

"No," said Timmy. "I suppose it's rather silly really, isn't it?"

"Yes," said Frog. Then seeing the sad look on his friend's face, he added, "Er, I mean No. No, it isn't silly at all. No sillier than taking a ticket in a raffle at the village whist drive. Tell you what we'll do, we'll both hang our stockings up and see what happens, shall we?"

"Oh, yes," said Timothy excitedly. "Do let's. As you say, you never know. As a matter of fact, I *did* find a biscuit in mine once—well, a bit of one anyway. I rather think a mouse left it there though, because it was a bit bitten. Have you got a stocking without a hole in, Froggy?"

"Yes, I think so. Let's go and have a look, shall we? Turn out the lights, old man. We'll raid the larder on the way up. I could do with a hunk of cheese and a biscuit." So saying, he led the way through the dark corridors to the kitchen, whistling as he went.

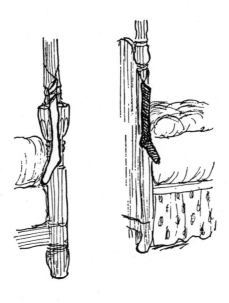

CHAPTER FOUR

The Visitor

TIMMY WAS so excited that night that he couldn't sleep at all. First he shut one eye and then the other, and then both, but the effort of keeping them *both* shut all the time was so terrific that he had to give it up. He counted sheep going through a gate and then found that they kept going through two and sometimes three at a time, so he had to take them all back, shut the gate and start all over again. Then he started counting hippopotamuses and that became dangerous as the hippopotamuses got longer and larger, and started dancing hornpipes all round the room.

"Bother," said Timmy to himself. "It must have been the plum cake, or," he added regretfully, "the punch." So he got out of bed and walked round the room several times to see if that would do any good.

Then through the window there came a little tinkling sound. He could hear it distinctly. At first it might have been the rustling of dead leaves against the window-pane, but then it got louder and louder until it came to a stop somewhere right above his head.

Timmy tiptoed out into the passage and down the stairs very quietly. His heart was hammering like a traction engine. Suddenly there was a noise like a gun going off. "Boom—Boom—Boom." Timmy bounded up the stairs two at a time and shot into bed and pulled the clothes up over his head and lay there suffocating and panting for breath, not daring to move.

"What was that?" Visions of ghosts and strange unnumbered things which walk in the night to frighten tortoises loomed up in his mind's eye. Then the old grandfather clock at the bottom of the stairs began to strike. One . . . two . . . three . . . four . . . five . . . six . . . seven . . . eight . . . nine . . . ten . . . eleven . . . twelve. "How stupid of me!" thought Timothy, it was only the clock. "But then," he thought, "that wasn't the only noise—I heard another sort of tinkly sound, distinctly."

Unable to restrain himself a moment longer, he

tiptoed once again to the door and listened. Yes, there it was again. Tinkle . . . tinkle . . . plink. Tinkle . . . tinkle . . . plink. Pushing his feet into his worn-out slippers, Timmy slipper-sloppered down the stairs again, his heart hammering so hard against his ribs that he felt sure it must burst through.

The noise seemed to come from the great hall and yet somehow it sounded very far away. As he neared the center of the hall, a sudden gust of wind rattled down the chimney and blew his candle out "whoosh." At that Timmy's old heart failed him altogether and he dropped the candle and started to run in the direction of where he thought the door was.

Instead, he ran straight into the fireplace and fell headlong over one of the huge iron "dogs" which stood guard like sentinels over Frog's fireplace. He landed in a heap on his back on a pile of smoldering ash. "Bother," said Timmy. "Bother," and "Help," and "Oh, dear!" said Timmy as he felt the tender underneath part of him start to scorch on the cinders. It was difficult to get up if you were a tortoise and found yourself in this position. He was struggling hard, puffing, panting, and wriggling, and getting hotter and hotter when the most EXTRAORDINARY thing happened.

To Timmy it felt as if the end of the world had come. Indeed, he quite expected it and was preparing himself quite solemnly to pay the penalty for being a too inquisitive tortoise. (Although, during the interval of wriggling away from one particular hot bit of ash before finding himself next to an equally hot bit, he couldn't help thinking that roasting alive was rather a big price to pay for a little extra inquisitiveness on Christmas Eve.) . . .

And then IT happened. To this day Timmy is unable to remember really how IT happened. All he remembers is that at one minute, there he was, smouldering gently away on the fire. The next minute there he was . . . or thought he was, but wasn't quite sure because his immediate world, which he was preparing to become gradually roasted out of, was suddenly blotted out by an enormous mountain. This descended from somewhere above him and landed in a bellowing, struggling heap all over him and the fire and the ashes, sending clouds of dust in every direction.

"Bodkins," grunted the THING. "Bulbous bodkins and buckets of blood!"

"Bulbous bodkins and buckets of blood!"

"Ow!" yelled Timmy. "Help! Ow! HELP!" But
for all the noise he made he might have been a worm
wrapped up in an eiderdown.

The THING, whatever IT was, cursed and struggled
and puffed and blew until it finally worked itself
out of the fire and on to the hearth rug, meanwhile,
unintentionally, pushing poor old Timmy farther
back into the ashes. His shell began to crack and

fizzle like a roasting chestnut. "Ow! Ow! Ow!" he yelled. "HELP! HELP! HELP!"

The THING, which by now had resolved itself into a gruff voice in the darkness, shouted, "Where are you, whoever you are? How can I help you if I don't know where you are?"

"I'm in the fire," squeaked Timmy. "Quick, quick or I won't be me any more."

"Dear, oh dear!" muttered the VOICE. "I wish I could see. Pusskin! Pusskin! Where are you?"

"Mee . . . ow! Here I am," said another voice, only a much smaller squeakier one this time.

"Well, hurry up then. You can see in the dark. Find this 'WHO-IS-IT' and get it out of the fire. I've lost my SPECIAL SPECS down this wretched chimney somewhere and I can't seen a thing."

"Mee . . . ow," answered Pusskin and before he knew what had happened a soft furry paw came and pushed Timmy gently over on to his front again so that he was able to scuttle out of the fire quite easily.

"Pouff!" puffed Timmy, blowing the ashes out of his nose. "Thank you. Pouff! Pouff!"

Then, from high up on the mantelpiece, on to which he had jumped, Pusskin threw down a box of matches. By the light of a single match Timmy sud-

denly saw something which made his heart turn a
double somersault, and he toppled over backwards
again. Great heavens! It was Father Christmas himself. Red cloak, white whiskers and all!

"Dear me! He's on his back again, Pusskin! Here,
old fellow, let me help you." And the kindly old gentleman bent down and rolled Timmy gently on to his
feet once more.

"Thank you, thank you," muttered the poor overcome tortoise, blushing through his partly-burnt
shell. "You have saved my life. I f-f-fell into the f-f-
fire and would have been roasted to death if it
hadn't been for you and your kind cat."

"Oh, never mind that!" said Father Christmas.
"All in a night's work, you know. Tell me, what is
this place? How do I get out of here?"

"Oh!" answered Timmy quickly. "This is Frogmorton Hall. It belongs to my friend Frederick
Frog," he added.

"Any children here?"

"No," said Timmy. "Er—I mean yes. . . . Well,
no, not exactly," he added regretfully.

By this time old Father Christmas had got a candle burning bravely and saw by the light of it the
look of dreadful disappointment on poor Timothy's
face.

"Er—hem," he said, clearing his throat and pulling his beard thoughtfully. "It's not on my list. Must have come down the wrong chimney. Fell down it in fact. Never known such a great hole of a place. Might have broken my neck. Funny thing," he said, "haven't mistaken a chimney like that for years. Are you sure there aren't any children here? Must have been dozens here once, I should say. I can almost hear their little feet dancing round the old hall playing 'Blind-man's-buff' and things —not so very long ago either."

"Oh, yes," put in Timothy eagerly. "There have been children here. Lots of them—only this evening. What a jolly time we had! They've all gone now, though," he added sadly. "Back to their little homes to wait for you."

"Yes, and I mustn't disappoint them either," said the old man in red, "I'm late as it is. Here! Give us a hand with this sack and see if you can find my specs, Pusskin."

"Mee—ow, mee—ow," came a faint voice from somewhere up the chimney where Pusskin was already searching for the precious missing spectacles.

"Y-you c-can't go back up the chimney again," cried Timothy earnestly. "It's much too steep and dangerous. Look, I'll show you the way to the front door. That is if you *must* go so soon," he added regretfully. "I'm sure Froggy would have loved to meet you, but he's fast asleep, and I don't think we ought to wake him."

He helped heave the heavy sack on to Father Christmas's back. This was a very hard and tiring business for a very small tortoise, and as he was pushing away with all his might a big shiny whistle and a bright red mouth-organ fell out of the top and landed almost on his head.

Now a mouth-organ was something which Timothy had longed for all his life and had never possessed and there it lay all bright red and shining and wrapped in celophane paper at his feet, and the whistle beside it glistening in the candlelight. Oh, beautiful, dream-like things! The temptation was too great. Timmy said nothing. Father Christmas obviously hadn't heard them drop. Timmy picked them up and shoved them deep into his dressing-gown pocket.

A queer prickly feeling like a sudden rush of measles flooded all over him. Timmy had a guilty conscience. All the same, he still kept his hand crushed hard over the mouth-organ and the whistle and guided Father Christmas through the

The reindeer was standing in the snow, his nose very red with the cold

old, dark passages by the light of a candle until they got to the front door. There Rudolph the Reindeer was standing in the snow, his nose very red with the cold, and Pusskin was already sitting in her place with Father Christmas's spectacles which she had rescued from the chimney clutched firmly in one paw.

"Well, well, we must be on our way now," began Father Christmas.

"Er—er—wait a minute," stammered Timothy and dived back again into the house, reappearing again several minutes later with a tray laden with biscuits and cheese and a small jar of ginger wine, which had somehow escaped getting swallowed up at the party.

"These are Frog's really, of course," said Timmy, "but I know he would want you to have them. After all, people are usually asleep when you come, so they can't give you anything, can they?"

"No," said the old man, shaking his head, "we don't often get anything nice like this, do we, Pusskin? People don't often think of giving old Father Christmas anything. They usually expect him to bring *them* something. But there's one house we go to on top of a hill, it's a very poor little house. An old lady and a little girl live there and every year they leave a currant bun and a glass of milk out for me, and I can't tell you how grateful I am for it after a hard night's work.

"And now we really must be going," he said at last as he brushed the crumbs off his curly white beard and shook out the folds of his cloak in the frosty starlight. "Will you thank your friend Mr. Frog very much indeed for his kind hospitality? I won't forget it. Now then, Pusskin, is everything on board?"

And then a funny little voice which seemed to come out of Timmy's pocket shouted, "Wait!" It was Timmy's voice really, but it felt as if it were coming out of his pocket. It was his voice and yet he couldn't hear himself saying anything. The mouth-organ! Perhaps it had been meant for that little girl who lived on top of the hill and always remembered old Father Christmas. And the whistle, that, too, had been meant for some boy or girl equally important, and they might be the last to be visited and nothing would be left in the sack, and all because a HORRID, GREEDY, OLD TORTOISE . . .

Father Christmas was cracking his whip, in another second it would be too late.

Suddenly like a bubbling stream breaking over a boulder, the words poured out of Timmy's mouth. "Oh, Father Christmas, wait!" he spluttered. "Please wait! Y-y-you dropped these out of your sack. I p-picked them up, they g-g-got into my pocket and I m-m-meant . . ."

Old Father Christmas held up his hand trying to stop the flow of agonizing confession which was pouring from Timmy's lips. "Don't worry, old fellow," he said gently, "I know you wanted the mouth-organ, that's why I dropped it; *keep it,* and the whistle will do for your kind friend to whistle his dog with. If you hadn't mentioned picking them up, the mouth-organ would just have melted away in your pocket, but the whistle would have stayed there to remind you that I never forget anything. You're a good kind tortoise and in future I'll call on you every Christmas because there are some people who, fortunately, never grow up and you're one of them. Good-bye, Timothy Tortoise, and God bless you!"

Then as Timmy raised his paw to his eye, to wipe away a great big tear that had got stuck there, there was a flurry of bells and snow, and he was gone, and all that remained was a few crumbs of bread and cheese on a plate, an empty ginger wine jar, the precious mouth-organ and whistle clutched in his paw, and the sleigh marks in the snow. He turned and walked slowly back into the house.

A shooting star shot like an arrow through the sky and the old wind sighed a whispering sigh in the cedar trees, remembering so many long-forgotten Christmases.

CHAPTER FIVE

The Morning After

IT WAS a sort of crispy-crackly-rattling noise somewhere down in the region of his toes that awoke
Timothy Tortoise on Christmas morning. The more
he wriggled his toes the more the "whatever-it-was"
crackled. He couldn't understand it. Of course any
reasonably intelligent child of four could have told
him what it was, but Timmy was an old tortoise unaccustomed for too many years to the mysteries of
Christmas and he was baffled.

It was still very dark, so he struck a match, lit
the candle by his bed and held it in one shaky
paw while he groped down to the end of the bed
with the other. And there it was. His stocking
was tied round the bedpost with somebody's old
bootlace and it was bursting and brimming over
with exciting things. Poor old Timmy just sat

A stocking full and overflowing and all for him

there staring at it, rubbing his tired old eyes and
hardly daring to breath. Surely if he looked away
for an instant it would vanish into thin air. He
blinked and shook his head. No. It was still there.
How amazing. A stocking full and overflowing and
all for him. It was just too wonderful to believe.

Then, like someone waking from a dream he began to remember the events of the past night. The party and then the extraordinary encounter with Father Christmas. His skin prickled at the very memory of the narrow escape he had had in the red-hot ashes of the fire. It was all so bewildering that things like that could happen to *him,* a poor old partially-forgotten tortoise.

Putting the candle down on the table, he untied his stocking and brought the glorious thing nearer to the light. Oh, joy! There were two big crackers in the top—and then farther down two green and white striped lollipop sticks and a toy trumpet. "Toot . . . Toot . . . Toot," went Timmy, almost delirious with excitement. Then, a box of cough drops (very handy), a large red cotton handkerchief, a piece of shaving soap, a toothbrush (silly, because Timmy only had two teeth), a bag of nuts, a small calendar, an orange, a tin of tiny little biscuits like you find in dolls' houses, two rather sticky peppermints, and best of all, a beautiful shiny new trowel with a green handle, right at the bottom. And then, of course, at the very toe, was a lump of coal done up in purple paper.

What a wonderful stocking-full. Timmy pushed everything back again and hurried along to Frog's room to show him the glorious wonder of it all. He bounced on Frog's bed in a fit of terrific excitement.

"Wake up, wake up, Froggy," he shouted. "Father Christmas has been here and he's filled our stockings. Look! Here's yours. Full up to the brim like mine. Oh, do wake up, Froggy, old man! It's Christmas Day."

"Grumph," muttered Frederick Frog and rolled ponderously on to his back. "Zzzzzzz . . . pfffff . . ." he snored.

Timmy was exasperated. He tried tweaking Frog's toes under the bedclothes, bouncing up and down on the bed all the while singing, "Wake up, Froggy. Wake up, Froggy. It's Christamus, Christamus, Christmas Day," until he was quite exhausted. Finally, he pulled both Frog's ears very hard. That did it.

"What the jumping Jehoshaphats are you doing?" Frog shouted angrily, when he had recovered from his fright. "It's the middle of the night."

"No, no, it's not," said Timmy. "It's six o'clock in the morning and it's Christmas Day, and Father Christmas has been here. He came down the big chimney in the hall and landed on top of me, and pulled me out of the fire—or at least his cat did, and he left me a mouth-organ and you a whistle, and

then he must have filled our stockings *somehow,*
but I never saw him go upstairs and I'm sure mine
wasn't full when I went up to bed—at least, I don't
remember seeing it, and then he got into his sleigh
and 'whoosh' he was gone. Just like that. Oh, yes!
And I gave him some bread and cheese and a jar of
ginger wine. I thought you wouldn't mind, and I
didn't wake you up because I thought you'd be cross
and——"

"You're jolly well right, I would," said Frog vehe-
mently. "I'm jolly well cross now. Waking a fellah
up in the middle of the night. Babblin' about Father
Christmas. Carryin' on like a child of two. Robbin'
a chap of his beauty sleep. You've been dreamin'.
That's what's the matter with you. Go back to bed
like a good chap and we'll talk about it in the morning, shall we? I'm tired."

"But it is the morning, Froggy—Christmas morning," pleaded Timothy. "Do wake up and look at
your stocking. Just to please me. *Please,* Froggy."
Frog was a very, very kind person and he simply
hated hurting people's feelings, so with much heav-
ing and grunting he got himself into a sitting position.

"All right," he yawned; "but I still don't believe
all this nonsense. Father Christmas wouldn't bother

his head with two worn-out old fogies like us. He's got too many children to go and call on. He's a busy man. He's . . ." Then he blinked and rubbed his eyes. There, sure enough, at the bottom of his bed was a bulky, bulging object which bore little or no relation to the long, thin, limp golf stocking which he had put there (only to please his friend Tortoise) the night before.

"God bless my soul!" exclaimed Froggy. "What an astoundin' thing. My stockin' 's bin filled up! Would you believe it!"

"That's what I've been trying to tell you," put in Timmy excitedly. "Oh, do open it quickly."

"Orl right, orl right," said Frog. "Don't bustle me. Hate being bustled at this time in the morning." But he was almost as excited as Timmy really, and his fingers shook as he unwrapped the paper and colored string from a small box which contained six sticks of different colored sealing-wax.

"Well, well," he exclaimed. "How thoughtful of Father Christmas! I can never find any sealing-wax and now I've got six whole sticks of it, a different color for every day except Sunday. And what's this?" By this time he had pulled out a balloon, an orange, a bag of nuts and some liquorice all-sorts and had come to another little box, flat like a cigarette tin. "Oh! Timmy, look! A box of flies for my new fishing-rod. Who would have thought of that? How simply splendid!" And now he had got to the bottom—there was the lump of coal. "Very useful too," muttered Froggy to himself. "Timmy, where are you?" he shouted.

But Timmy was rushing back to his room again to fetch Frog *his* present and the silver dog whistle. He returned out of breath and thrust them into Freddy's lap.

"Many happy Christmas—er—Christmases," muttered Timmy, breathlessly and rather mixed up. "Here is Father Christmas's present and here is mine."

"Oh! I say! Thank you very much, old chap. Jolly decent of you to think of me. And what a splendid present! A sponge bag! How did you know I needed a new one? Mine is as old as the hills. A *red* one too. My favorite color. What a clever old tortoise you are!" Frog was clearly delighted with both his presents.

After about half an hour discussing all the events of the previous night and the contents of their stockings, Frog began to get impatient for his breakfast.

"Come on, Timmy," he said. "Let's go and cook our own. Mrs. Grubbins won't be ready with it for another hour, at least. She doesn't come in to call us till half-past seven."

So the two animals dressed hurriedly and pattered downstairs to the kitchen where Timmy tied on an apron which he found hanging behind the door (Mrs. Grubbins's probably), and took charge of the operations. He was quite used to cooking, having no one else to do it for him in his own little flat in London. Very soon four long bacon rashers were frizzling in the pan and two duck eggs beside them, and the smell was simply scrumptious.

After breakfast Timmy put on a pair of galoshes which he'd found in the lobby, an old pair which somebody had left behind, and Frog put on his long boots, and armed with two stout sticks, they sallied forth into the frosty, sunshiny morning.

"Look, Froggy!" squeaked Timothy, pointing at the snow as they stepped carefully off the last step into the broad carriage sweep. It was very slippery and both of them wanted to avoid falling. (A fall at their time of life could be quite a serious matter.) "Look! There's Father Christmas's sleigh marks in the snow . . . and . . . and look, there's Rudolph's . . ."

"Rudolph? Who's Rudolph?" interrupted Frog.

"Rudolph the Red-nosed Reindeer of course," said Timmy. "Now don't you tell me you haven't heard of *him.*"

"Never knew there was such a person," said Frog. "Really, Timmy, I think you're getting a little light in the head. . . . A reindeer with a red nose. Sure your old imagination ain't gettin' a bit the best of you? Reindeers don't have red noses. At least none of the ones *I* know," he added quickly, looking round rather suspiciously. "Honestly, old boy, I think the moon must have got into your head."

"Well! If you don't believe me, look at *that* then," said Timmy, pointing victoriously with his stick to several large footprints in the snow, like soup plates with a chunk out of them.

"Hmmmm-mm," muttered Frog, half to himself. "Those *are* reindeer's feet or I'm a Dutchman. Yes, they're either reindeer's feet or dynosoruses, but they couldn't be dynosoruses because they're all dead."

"What's a dynosorusus?" asked Timmy.

"It's an ancient animal that used to go galumphin' about frightenin' people," said Frog, "but nobody's seen one for years and years and years, so it can't be one of those. Deduction: It must be your old reindeer, Timmy, old boy, but I'm not havin' the red-nosed one. That's a bit too much."

"Well," said Timmy, "it *was* a red-nosed one and shiny too—just like a beacon. I *saw* it, so I know. Look!" he said suddenly, pointing again with his stick in great excitement. *"There* now, you disbelieving old animal. See that deep little round hole in the snow—there, by the big scuffled-about bit? That's where he put his nose while he was lying about waiting. He *breathed* that hole in the snow with his big red nose," he added triumphantly.

"*Orl* right, *orl* right. Have it your own way then," conceded Frog, with a good-natured smile. "It was Rufus, the reindeer with a red nose."

"Rudolph," corrected Timmy.

"Very well, Rudolph then. Now let's go and have a look at the ducks before it's time to come back and get ready for church."

CHAPTER SIX

A Strange Christmas Day

THE DUCKS had organized a skating party. As Frog and Timmy approached they could hear the merry "quack-quack-quacking," and see all the ducks sliding about and having a high old time.

"Halloa, over there," shouted Frog. "Merry Christmas to you."

"Merry Christmas," quacked all the ducks. "Quackie-quack-quack." And went on sliding. Only about two of the older ones were any good at it and most of them slipped and slithered about helplessly looking rather silly. But they were all enjoying it very much.

Frog and Timmy stood on the sheltered side of a great big clump of bulrushes so that they were hidden from the other side of the pond although they could see everything that was going on.

Suddenly there was a warning. "Quaa—ck," from one of the old ducks, who had been quietly circling round on the farther side, trying to do a figure of eight on his own. "Quaa—ck," he shouted again,

The ducks had organized a skating party

this time with a deep, resonant note. This meant DANGER. All the other ducks stopped or somehow slithered to a standstill and stood like sentinels, their little black beady eyes expressionless—waiting.

Then in an instant it seemed as though the whole pond was moving. What had been an expanse of shining white ice, covered with a thin layer of powdery snow, bright and glistening in the morning sun, had in a single breathless moment become a moving, wriggling mass of little brown and grey bodies—RATS!

Immediately the ducks rose into the air circling

the pond, their pond, Frog's pond, which had been attacked so hideously on this bright Christmas morning. But one or two of them were caught. Too old to act instantly, their old legs rheumaticky and infirm, they had been pounced upon by a menacing grey circle of destruction and willful murder. The stoats at this moment joined forces with the rats, knowing that most of the work had already been done. One of them sprang on to the back of an old drake and hung there, his sharp little teeth embedded in the dark-green feathers.

For a split second Frog was at a loss to know what to do. Then, as so often happens in the moment of grave danger, his long line of brave, blue-blooded ancestors stood him in good stead. His great-great-great-grandfather, who fought with Wellington at Waterloo, his thirteen-times great uncle who helped Drake repulse the Armada, suddenly became reincarnated in Frog himself as he barked out orders to Timothy in a short, staccato, military voice.

"Run back to the house as fast as you can. Bring the guns. Tell Harold the Hunter to gallop into the village and bring as many men as he can muster. Matt and I will try and hold the pond until you get back." And with that he strode on to the ice into full view of the enemy, the faithful Matt following closely at his heels, sniffing and whining and letting out short yelps of excitement, awaiting the moment when Frog would allow him to charge.

The rats were taken by surprise. They hadn't expected any opposition and the sudden appearance of Frog, a small but very belligerent figure in duffel coat and gum boots, carrying his big, thick ash plant, followed by his dog, caused them to drop their quarry and turn, uncertain for a moment whether to stand or run. But they were hungry and the old ducks still stood there as if rooted to the ground, piteously quacking—half a dozen great fat dinners on legs, food for rats and stoats for weeks and weeks to come.

It was a great big grandfather rat who rallied them with an imperial twitch of his great long whiskers. They obeyed him, fanning out into a wide semi-circle across the pond, flanked on one side by the stoats, who kept the poor old ducks prisoners between themselves and the slowly advancing Frog, mesmerising them with their wicked little eyes.

It was clear to Frog that, with the odds so enormously against him, his only hope lay in playing for time and praying that Timmy would get back before the rats launched their main attack on him. Against their enormous numbers he and Matt would be completely powerless in the end. Although Matt had already accounted for twenty or more, making short scurries in among their ranks, biting and snapping and retreating again to guard his master, whom he daren't leave for long, armed as he was with only his stout ash plant and his enormous courage. The old dog's teeth were not so good as they used to be though, and he took longer finishing off a rat than he would have done in his younger days.

So far, Frog and Matt had been slowly advancing. Frog, walking very slowly, his chest stuck out, brandishing his stick like a sword in front of him, Matt dashing backwards and forwards along the line, making short, sharp raids here and there, his tail waving like a banner behind him. But Frog with his keen military instinct could tell that the tide would soon turn. There were too many rats. More and more seemed to be coming from nowhere to take the places of those who had fallen. The ranks of grey and brown bodies seemed to be swelling visibly all the time.

Now, after each sortie into the enemy ranks, Matt glanced uneasily over his shoulder at his master. The rats were barely retreating. at all. They just wriggled a little, first one way and then the other, but they weren't giving away any ground now. The long grey line remained intact. The point of climax had been reached.

Frog was worried. Would Timmy never come with those precious guns? It seemed as if he and Matt had been fighting this grim battle for a year, not for just a quarter of an hour. Matt was getting tired too. His breath came in short, hard pants and his long pink tongue lolled out of his mouth dripping hot water on to the ice.

"Le—ooo in there, old fella," shouted Frog, encouraging his old servant with his firm friendly voice. "Le—ooo in. Bite 'em. Kill 'em. Hav' at 'em, ole boy. Good dog. Good boy."

But he knew with an awful certainty that unless help came within the next few minutes their number was up and they would be pounced on and torn to pieces by a howling, shrieking mob of slithering grey and brown shapes. Frog's tongue went dry and stuck to the roof of his mouth.

"This is it," he thought to himself as he finally came face to face with one enormous rat who seemed to be the leader of the whole army. It grinned and bared its teeth at him. He found, oddly enough, that he was much more angry than frightened. Angry that the life that he enjoyed so much was about to come to an abrupt end. Angrier still that this, his home, the home of the Fitzherbert Frogs for fifteen generations, would be invaded by this filthy, ill-mannered mob and probably lived in by them and their disgusting families and he, Frederick, dead and unable to do anything about it. Either that or it would be sold and that dreadful Mountebank Goad would buy it. The thought was too awful to contemplate. Frog brandished his stick, yelling at the top of his voice, "Tarrara boom di ai. Slash 'em, bash 'em, cut 'em in strips."

"Grrr—rr," growled Matt, and made another dash into the fray, returning with two dead rats and blood dripping from his nose.

But now, although he daren't look round, Frog knew that they were encircled on all sides and the great-grandfather rat just sat and stared at him— grinning, waiting for the end.

All this while, Timmy, having run as hard as his poor old legs would carry him back to the house for the guns and to give the warning, was wrestling with the lock on Frog's gun case. Try as he would,

"Slash 'em, bash 'em, cut 'em in strips"

he couldn't get it open and he couldn't find Frog's keys anywhere. Mrs. Grubbins was out. In desperation he rushed into the library. Alas! the big glass cupboard in which Frog's old guns were kept was locked. Timmy picked up a heavy boot and threw it with all his force at the cupboard. The glass shattered and he hauled out two of these fierce-looking weapons.

"Cartridges," thought Timmy, "I wonder where he keeps them?" He dashed back again into the lobby. There he found a big wooden box with a large label on it THIS SIDE UP. HANDLE WITH CARE. "These must be cartridges," thought Timmy, bash-

ing on the box with a hammer and chisel. And sure
enough they were. Timmy crammed as many as he
could into his pockets, which had been mercifully
sewn up by Mrs. Grubbins, and shuffled into the
hall, shouldering the two heavy guns as he went.
The weight of them was terrific. It bore him down
so that he was bent double.

Shouldering the two heavy guns as he went

Then an awful thing happened. As he reached the head of the steps, leading down into the drive, his foot slipped and he fell headlong, guns and all, LUMPITY, WUMPITY, BUMP to the bottom. Stars and stripes and balls of fire leapt before his eyes and then everything went black and he rolled on to his back, a poor little unconscious tortoise on the stony gravel drive.

CHAPTER SEVEN

The Rescue

How long Timmy would have lain there I don't know if Harry the Hunter hadn't suddenly appeared, galloping headlong down the drive, bearing on his back Bill Badger, Otto the Otter, Sammy Squirrel, and old Robert the Rabbit, who had somehow or other scrambled up behind, refusing to be left out of anything.

"Whoa, boy," shouted Bill Badger as they rounded the bend which brought them into Frog's carriage sweep. "There's Frog's friend, Timothy Tortoise. Looks as though he's had an accident. Here, give me a hand." And he slipped down off the tall back of Harry the Hunter, helped by an outstretched paw from Otto the Otter.

"Mmmm—mm," muttered the old badger under his breath. "Bad case of concussion, I should say.

Galloping headlong down the drive

Trying to carry those guns down the steps, silly old idiot. Should have waited for help. We can't leave 'im lying here like this. Can't shift 'im, though. May 've broken some bones. What d'you think we'd better do, Otto?"

Otto, who never spoke, unless it was absolutely necessary, was above all a practical person of profound knowledge and common sense. If ever he said anything, you could be sure it would be worth listening to. That is why all the animals went to him for advice.

"Well," said Otto in his slow deliberate voice,

"Tortoise may *look* uncomfortable, but he's alive and in no serious danger. Frog on the contrary *is*. Therefore, I would suggest leaving Tortoise with a coat over him to keep him warm, and taking the guns with all possible speed to the scene of action."

And this is what they did. Otto and Bill Badger climbed back on to the back of Harry the Hunter, each grasping a heavy gun in one hand while managing somehow or other to cling on with the other. And everyone, except Robert the Rabbit, who'd lent his coat to act as a rug for the prostrate Timmy, stuffed his pockets with as many cartridges as he could carry.

Faster and faster galloped Harry, who was no Derby winner at the best of times, but realized the urgency of the errand that he was on, and bumpity-bumpity-bump went everybody, manfully endeavouring not to fall off. Poor old Robert the Rabbit was in the worst position, being on the propelling end, and if it hadn't been for Sammy Squirrel's bushy tail which he clung to with all the desperation of a shipwrecked sailor clinging to a raft, he would most certainly have bitten the dust many, many times.

At last they sighted the pond, almost hidden among the bulrushes and weeds, and now it was impossible for Harry the Hunter to go any farther. He was already sinking well above his knees in the boggy ground. "Dismount," whispered Bill Badger, who had automatically taken control, being the largest (and bossiest) member of the party. All four animals slid to the ground, which was much closer now and quite nice squashy falling.

"Hold your fire till we get to the very edge of the pond and can see where you're aiming. We don't want to hit Frog by mistake."

Now they crept forward as silently as they could. Poor Robert had a severe attack of hiccoughs after his bumpy ride and had to bury his head in the muddy water every few yards to stifle his "hicks," with the result that he was very out of breath and panting like a grampus at the end of the line. "Ssssh," hissed everybody at once and a snipe rose out of the bog, giving the alarm.

Poor Frog with Matt at his side, now completely surrounded in a tiny circle at the very center of the pond, which was covered so thickly with rats and stoats *and* weasels that it would have been impossible to put a pin between them, heard it and hardly dared to believe his ears. Could it be help coming? The snipe wheeled high into the air, making a curious drumming sound and then dived almost on to Frog's head and piped as loud as it could in a little shrill voice.

"Mr. Frog, Mr. Frog, your friends are here."

Frog had been spending these last few moments, which seemed like endless hours while his enemies had been preparing for the kill, praying that now that his time had come, he would die true to the old Fitzherbert Frog tradition, silently, without even so much as a squeak.

There was now only a matter of about ten inches between himself and the nearest rat, and Matt was lying about another foot away trying to prop his eyes open with his paws, his tongue lolling out of his mouth like a great red river, so tired he was completely unable to move. And the rats still waited, like vultures, for the final scene, savoring the last moments before the end, giving their victims plenty of time to imagine the full horror of what that end would be.

The friendly snipe flew back again to the bulrushes where Bill Badger and the others were still creeping forward, clutching the heavy guns. "Hurry, hurry, hurry," it shrilled, drumming as hard as it could with its wings. "They're surrounded and the rats are ready to eat them. There's no time to lose."

Just at that moment, Bill Badger, in his anxiety

to get through the rushes, put his foot on a slimy stone, slipped, and his gun, which was cocked and ready for action, went off with a tremendous BANG! which sent all the animals reeling over backwards into the swampy undergrowth.

The rats on the pond looked over their shoulders uneasily, but they were still bent on destroying Frog and Matt and the six helpless old ducks, which they had now got penned into a tiny cavity in the rocks at the farthest end of the pond, bundled on top of one another in a pathetic heap, quacking feebly at intervals.

Bill Badger and Otto Otter now burst through the last big patch of rushes surrounding the pond and fired simultaneously into the midst of the enemy. Panic ensued. Rats and stoats started to run in all directions, except the old grandfather rat whose name was Hamish the Horrible. He was as deaf as a post. He had poor Frog pinned between his terrible claws and was just about to tear him to pieces with his three remaining teeth, which were the size of razor blades and just as sharp. But he had reckoned without Matt, Frog's faithful friend and warrior. The old dog having had a few moments in which to recover from his complete state of exhaustion, was just able to drag himself the few necessary

Hamish the Horrible

feet across the ice and he made one last desperate grab at the long scaly tail of Hamish the Horrible and held fast.

At this dramatic moment, with a great clanging of bells, the village fire-engine arrived on the scene, manned by every available citizen of Frogmorton. The battle was over. The rats ran in every direction only to meet a hail of fire from Bill Badger and his party at one side of the pond or to fall headlong into the enormous cracks which were now appearing everywhere on the other side, caused by the great weight of the fire-engine.

Foster the friendly Fox drove the big red machine

fearlessly to the other side of the pond, although the ice was splintering and cracking in all directions. Once having gained the opposite bank, however, he and the other firemen quickly got to work unrolling the hose pipes, which they turned upon the fleeing rats and stoats to add the finishing touch to their final destruction.

It was a wonderful victory. A resounding and complete victory, snatched, as it were, from the very jaws of defeat. From the six or seven hundred rats, stoats *and* weasels (who had joined in at the very end, meaning to share the spoils) there remained but seven altogether, including, unfortunately,

The village fire-engine arrived on the scene

Hamish the Horrible, who had managed to get away minus his tail which Matt had bitten off. The remainder had been shot, drowned or hosed to death, to say nothing of the quite considerable number accounted for by Matt in the earlier stages of the battle.

The old ducks were safe now. Slowly they waddled back on to the pond and sat down thankfully on a large island of ice, which remained still uncracked in the very middle. Their more active friends and relations who had been circling and wheeling round, watching the whole proceedings safely from the air, gradually began to return one by one now that the danger was over.

The victors, several of them, wet and cold after having fallen once or twice into the icy water in pursuit of the last remnants of the rat army, now gathered on the bank side to await the return of the real heroes of the day, Frog and Matt. They were being rescued from the center of the pond by Foster the Fox and his fire-fighters with the aid of two long ladders jammed together and a rope. Bill Badger, of course, was superintending these operations.

"Steady there, Fox, old friend. Slowly does it. . . . Now another step, Froggy. . . . Your turn

now, Matt. . . . Pull, you fellows on the bank.
. . . Not so fast. . . . She's sinking at the other
end. . . . Hold on, you chaps. . . . Here, let me
give you a hand." Then with Otto the Otter holding his tail, they brought their combined weight to
bear on the landward end of the ladder which made
Frog's end give a sudden convulsive leap into the
air.

"Oi!" shouted Frog and Matt together as they
were lifted into the air clinging desperately to the
final rung of the ladder. They were both so tired
that any physical exertion at this stage was almost
too much for them. It looked as if they were both
going to drop off and fall though the treacherous,
cracking ice.

It was an anxious moment both for our heroes
and for their friends who were watching on the
bank.

Frog managed with a superhuman effort to haul
himself up through the rungs on to the top of the
ladder so that he sat astride one of the rungs, panting and very out of breath, but safe. Matt, however,
being very heavy and much less active, found this
feat quite impossible. There is no doubt that in
another minute the gallant old dog would have
dropped off and fallen straight through a great hole

in the ice directly beneath him and never been heard of again, if it hadn't been for a simply *splendid* thing that the ducks did. (And those of you who have ever thought of the duck as a rather brainless and feathered-headed creature, had better think again.)

Seeing the desperate plight that their friend and rescuer was in, the clever old things got into a huddle. The two fattest ones floated like a raft in the hole directly under the suspended Matt, while one by one the others climbed on one anothers' backs until they formed a sort of tower. When the last one was perched, Matt was able to stand on *his* back and hoist himself with much grunting on to the top of the ladder. The two animals then walked very carefully, so as not to fall through, all the way back to the bank where their friends were waiting to welcome them.

No film stars ever had a greater reception. There were hand-shakings and pattings on the back and, "Three cheers for Frog and his dog," again and again until Frog had to put a stop to it. He simply hated fuss of any sort.

Suddenly he looked round, and said: "Good heavens! Where's Timmy? Why isn't he here?"

Then Bill Badger and Otto told him what had happened to poor Timmy.

"Why on earth didn't you tell me before?" shouted Frog angrily. "We must go to him at once. The poor fellow's probably blue with cold by now. One of you should have stayed with him." He was really most put out.

So they all boarded the fire-engine and drove back as fast as it would go (which wasn't very fast, because it wasn't a very new model and went, CHUT . . . FIZZ . . . BANG! BANG . . . FIZZ . . . WALLOP! like an ancient dustbin, which annoyed Frog very much. Frog had never held with any kind of machine anyway, except, of course, his old Rolls Royce "Rolly" who was *quite* different).

"Bloomin' tin kettle," he kept muttering to himself, wondering all the time how his poor old friend was and whether they would get home to find him frozen to death.

But of course nothing of the kind had occurred. When they finally arrived at the house, there was no sign of Timmy and they finally found him in the gardener's cottage tucked up snugly in Mrs. Grubbins's shawl in a rocking chair with his toes toasting on Mrs. Grubbins's fender. And there also was Mrs. Grubbins herself, bustling about preparing hot soup in a great big saucepan.

So all the animals, large and small, somehow

managed to crowd into Mrs. Grubbins's kitchen until the late-comers overflowed into the parlor and they all sat down, some on chairs and some on the floor. Mrs. Grubbins and her little granddaughter Milly fed the whole lot with soup until they were all warm and comfy again, and they sang carols and swapped stories, and all agreed that it had been the most exciting Christmas they had ever had.

But Frog himself thanked Mrs. Grubbins very much for her kindness, and bidding the others "Good evening and a Happy Christmas," he and Matt trekked slowly home through the snow to their own fireside and a well-earned sleep.

CHAPTER EIGHT

A Bitter Blow

CHRISTMAS WAS OVER. That never-to-be-forgotten day of the famous Battle of Rats was now past history, and Frogmorton and its little village settled quietly back on its haunches again and life returned to normal. The snow disappeared. The first tentative buds appeared on the trees. The freezing blasts of winter with their sighing, moaning, hungry voices, gave way to the boisterous, blustering carefree winds of March.

What wonderful, happy days they were! But every now and then Timmy would get a horrid little gnawing feeling in the pit of his stomach and he would say hopelessly to Frog, "Froggy, old man, I really must go back to London. What will they be doing at the office without me? I'll go next week."

And Frog would say, "Nonsense, my dear old boy.

If they'd wanted you, they'd have sent you a telegram or something. Now don't fuss. You're doin' a splendid job of work here. Just look at the way the garden's improved since you came. I couldn't do without you now."

So that's the way the matter always rested, and Timmy was oh so happy to let it stay that way!

All day long, now that the frosts were out of the ground, he dug and weeded and hoed until his nails were worn right down to the quick, and even old Grubbins, seeing his enthusiasm, was fired with a desire to do something more than lean on his spade and chew tobacco. And the old garden shook itself and opened its arms to the spring with love and gladness, like a sailing ship returning to the sea.

The violets and the snowdrops, the little wild anemones, hidden for years under a heavy canopy of fusty old ivy, showed their shy faces. Daffodil shoots began appearing all over the place. The first primroses shone like stars on the banks leading down to the river and, when the thistles had been cut down in the park, great clumps of cowslips appeared, scenting the air with the heady, thrilling smell of spring.

But one day towards the middle of March, something happened which turned this earthly paradise into a place of gloomy foreboding, uncertainty, and despair.

It was as if a bride, happily expectant and dressed in a beautiful bridal gown, had suddenly been told that her wedding would not take place. And this was how it all came about.

One morning Frog went downstairs to give Matt his usual run in the garden before breakfast. (Timmy had a slight cold and so, having been given an aspirin the night before and a glass of hot whisky and lemon by the thoughtful Frog, had overslept himself. He slept very well now, you'll be glad to hear.) As Matt approached the foot of the great wide staircase, its beautiful red stair carpet now very worn and tattered, his hackles suddenly rose like a great ruff all round his head and, "Gr-r-r-rrr-phh," he said in his deepest, grumpiest voice.

There, seated on one of the high-backed chairs in the hall, was a sinister-looking character in a black overcoat, with his tail tucked underneath his arm and on his knees a big, black leather briefcase with a lock on it. It was Mr. Ferret, of Ferret, Ferret, Poke and Pry, the Inspector of Taxes.

"Good morning, Mr. Frog," he said in a high-pitched ferrety voice. "Rather cold for the time of year, don't you think?" And an icy, biting wind blew past him under the front door like a heralder of bad news.

"Yes," said Frog gruffly. "Might I ask, Ferret, what you're doin' in my house at this time in the mornin'? I haven't even had my breakfast yet."

"A little private matter, Mr. Frog," answered the ferret, smacking his skinny lips. "A question of unpaid income tax to the extent of thirteen thousand

It was Mr. Ferret of Ferret, Ferret, Poke and Pry, the Inspector of Taxes

pounds, nineteen shillings and seven-pence half-penny. But don't let me disturb your breakfast," he added ingratiatingly, "I can wait."

And so that was how Frog learned that for years and years taxes had been piling up that he knew nothing about. He wasn't a fellow with any head for business and so he had left all his financial affairs to his old friend and solicitor Horace Hare, who, unbeknown to him, had gone raving mad and thrown all his correspondence, bills, letters of credit, documents—everything, straight into the wastepaper basket, and gone to the dogs (greyhound racing of course). This may seem a very odd thing for a hare to do, but, you see, he was a *March* Hare.

It was a terrible blow. To say that it was a DISASTER is putting it mildly. Frog and Timmy sat woefully in the dining-room in front of their eggs and bacon and thought and thought and thought. "Cheer up, Timmy," Frog said at last, as he detected an enormous tear rolling down his old friend's cheek into his coffee. "You see, it could have been worse. I might have been a young fella with a family to look after, instead of an old codger gettin' on for seventy with all the best things behind 'im. I've had my life, Timmy, and if I have to spend the last few years in a workman's cottage in a row,

*All his correspondence, bills, etc., into the
wastepaper basket*

what does that matter? I shall still have old Matt
here and possibly you'll come and visit me from
time to time."

"Oh, Froggy," burst out Timmy, trying desper-
ately hard to smother his tears in his table napkin.
"Of course you must c-c-come and st-stay with *me*.
It's only a little p-p-poky flat in a back st-street

b-but it's my home and you're welcome to stay there for the r-rest of your life."

"Thank you, old chap," said Frog, patting him on the shoulder. "Very kind of you. I won't forget it, and if I can't get some sort of a job here, in the country, where I belong, I'll take you at yer word. But first I'll have to see about disposin' of this old place. There aren't many people who'll be wantin' a vast ole museum like this, these days. I know who will buy it, though, that dreadful Mountebank Sam Goad. He's been hankerin' after it for years. I'd like to see 'im in Hades first," he added through his teeth, in a sudden burst of anger.

"Froggy, you're so b-brave," stammered Timmy. "I know what it means to you and yet you can talk about it so calmly. To have to sell Frogmorton. Your home and the home of your ancestors for centuries. The Park! The trees! The garden! Oɴ, Froggy, isn't there *anything* we can do?"

"Nothin' short of a miracle, I'm afraid, and I never was much of a hand at those," Frog added with a suspicion of the old well-known twinkle in his eye. "Eat up your breakfast, there's a good fellah. We can't tackle all this on an empty stomach."

But Timmy, underneath his shell, was made of

softer stuff than his gallant companion. His eggs and bacon grew cold on his plate and he sat staring in front of him, his old hooded eyes misted over with salt tears. After a while, he got up, muttered a few unintelligible words and shuffled out into the garden still wearing his bedroom slippers.

There, under a great cedar tree, he paused and looked about him. The sun shone with a glorious early-morning brilliance, outlining everything with a halo of bright gold. The dew still hung in golden drops on spiders' webs between the branches. The grass beneath his feet was clipped and green (only yesterday he had brought the old mowing-machine out of its winter hiding-place and painstakingly mowed round the edges of the lawn in front of the house). Here and there in great clumps the first daffodils shook their lovely heads in the waving wind. Puffy white clouds raced, billowing across the bright-blue sky, like galleons in full sail, and in front of him the old house lay sleeping, its grey stone mellowed and turned to a dull gold by the slanting rays of the morning sun.

Timmy thought he had never seen it look more beautiful or more beloved. And the precious beauty of it all mocked the very birds that sang. He shuffled round and faced the other way, unable to bear the

He prayed for a miracle to happen

sight any longer. Then, as if moved by an instinct
stronger than himself, he stood clutching part of
the trunk of the old cedar tree, one of ten that had
been planted there by a Frog of Frogmorton six centuries before, and prayed for a miracle to happen.

CHAPTER NINE

Timothy Meets a New Friend

A s THE days went by Frog began to realize that his situation was pretty desperate.

He had been given six months in which to pay his taxes and when those six months were up, unless he could sell his house and land, it would mean bankruptcy, his name dishonored and disgraced. That to a Fitzherbert Frog was an unthinkable thing.

There was only one way out of it. He must swallow his pride and accept Samuel Goad's offer. What a bitter pill to have to gulp down!

Fourteen thousand pounds for the house and all the land, farms, and everything. It was what is called a knock-down price. Really quite ridiculous. But, what could he do? There was no alternative. His back was right up against the wall and Goad knew it. Already he had called at the house in his vulgar pale blue car covered in shining chromium plate, with his fat chauffeur at the wheel and his little fat wife, sitting propped up with cushions and covered with diamonds, sucking peppermints in the back.

The memory of the visit sent shudders down Frog's spine. "Funny old pile of a place," Goad had said. "Needs a lot done to it. The missus and I'll want a conservatory buildin' on and, of course, a lot more bathrooms and a nine-hole golf course. Must 'ave my round of golf every Sunday."

On and on he went, pulled the place to bits, knocking bits off there, building bits on there, until finally it seemed that none of the original old house, designed by one of the greatest architects of all time, would be left standing.

Frog glanced up at the beautiful fluted columns, at the bookshelves lined with his beloved leather-bound sporting books, the worn Persian rugs on the floor, the stern face of his ancestors gazing down from their gold frames as if anxious to help. But what could anyone do? All these things would have to be sold, and Goad would be standing here where Frog was now and there would be radio-gramophones all over the place and beastly modern furni-

All these things would have to be sold

ture instead of his dear old-fashioned comfy arm-chairs.

And still Frog hesitated before signing the fatal

document which would let the place pass out of his life for ever. He would do it to-morrow. Yes, he would do it to-morrow. He'd been saying that for the last six weeks and still the days went by.

Meanwhile, Timmy had been spending all his waking hours in the garden, digging, hoeing, and planting as if the devil were after him. He found that only by crawling into bed so unconscious with tiredness that he was sound asleep before he touched the pillow, was he able to escape the awful waves of self-pity and remorse which crept up like wicked demons to attack him during the night.

In the daytime he had to put up a brave show of indifference because Frog was being incredibly brave about the whole business, and after all he had so much more to lose. But lying in bed, in the dead of night, I'm ashamed to say poor old Timmy's courage waved him "Good-bye," and he cried as if his eyes would drop out. The more he tried to be brave and think of his noble friend Frog, the more his old enemies, Fear, Self-pity, and Remorse mustered themselves for the attack. "Oh, the lovely garden," they whispered. "You'll never see it again —or the greenhouses. Think of all those peaches on the walls which you've tended so carefully. Goad will eat them. You'll never see the color of one of them. Poor old Tortoise! What a terrible shame! And just as Life seemed to be beginning for you all over again." And poor Timmy dissolved into a squashy pulp. It was a wonder he didn't catch double pneumonia lying in an enormous puddle of his own tears.

And so every day he worked and worked and worked until his back felt as if it would break and his fingers were so worn that he couldn't possibly hold a teacup and had to drink out of a saucer. Old Grubbins, who had grown fond of "M*aa*ster Timmy," as he called him, became quite worried about him and finally spoke to Frog on the subject.

"Fair workin' 'isself to death, 'e be," he said. "An' all to no purpose. Hoi says to 'im, 'Whoi,' oi says, 'work yer pore fingers to the bone for the loiks o' that hupstart wots got no roight to be takin' Mr. Frederick's house and lands?' oi says. 'Better be a diggin' a nice toidy graave for 'e to loi in,' says oi."

But Frog with his knowledge of the world and its ways, just smiled, and said, "Better leave 'im be, Grubbins. Perhaps he knows best what he's doin' it for. We've all got to fight our own battles in our own peculiar fashion." So the old gardener just shook his head sadly as if to say that the world cer-

tainly seemed a topsy-turvy place and went on his
way, touching his cap respectfully as he went.

One evening, Timmy walked down to old Farmer
Crossbones's farm to collect the milk, because Mrs.
Grubbins's granddaughter Milly who usually did
it was away visiting her aunt. On the way back
he paused, leaning over a stile to pass the time of
day with a horse which stood in the corner of a
large field, hanging his head in a rather depressed
sort of way. This horse was a new arrival and
Timmy, in spite of all that had happened, hadn't
lost any of his old inquisitiveness.

"Evening, Horse," he said. "Nice fine evening it
is, too. Forgive me for addressing you as 'Horse' but
as we haven't been introduced, I'm afraid I don't
know your proper name."

"Well," answered the horse, "my name's of no importance. Not now, anyway," he added gloomily.
"It's a long story and I don't want to bother anybody with it. You just go on calling me 'Horse.'
Everybody else does. Even Harry the Hunter. I
don't mind. After all, it's better than being called
'Pig,' don't you think? Haw. . . . Haw. Funny
joke," he said, and then he opened his mouth and
yawned and it was easily the biggest yawn Timmy

had ever seen. As he stared down into that great cavern of a mouth Timothy was quite afraid and backed away. He was quite glad to be on the other side of the stile.

"Don't be afraid, little Tortoise," said Horse. "I didn't mean to be rude. As a matter of fact, I'm very partial to a little company. I get very lonely in this big field of an evening. They don't put one with the cows because they've got horns, and any-

He was quite glad to be on the other side of the stile

how," he added, "who ever got any sense out of a cow? They're the stupidest creatures imaginable. All they think about is eating and sleeping. Not that I blame them for that, mind you. But it's DULL, little Tortoise, it's immeasurably DULL." And he yawned again even wider this time, until Timmy thought that his jaws would certainly split in two.

"You see," he went on, "I'm used to rather a different life. Excitement. Color. Crowds. Thundering hooves. Glamor."

"Go on," stammered Timmy, quite excited. "I know. Hunting horns. Scarlet coats. The cry of hounds. The distant view of a fox. How well I can understand it! Years ago, you know—" he began . . .

"I don't know *what* you're talking about," interrupted Horse quite rudely. "Horses and hounds be blowed! I wasn't talking about hunting. I've *never* been a hunter." And poor Timmy, who realized that he'd put his foot in it once again, saw that his new-found friend was really quite indignant and upset.

"I'm a *racehorse,*" he said quite proudly and then he added quietly: "At least I was a racehorse—once." And he hung his head rather sadly and went on munching the daisies.

*   *   *

Timmy's inquisitiveness was now thoroughly roused. A real live RACEHORSE! Just think of it! Living at the bottom of the park! How terribly exciting! His ears flapped and grew all pink round the edges in his anxiety not to miss anything.

Although, at first, Horse seemed rather reluctant to discuss his past life, Timmy finally broke through his reserve or what appeared to be more a sort of bored indifference, and what he learned was really quite flabbergasting. He tucked away pieces of the exciting conversation into his memory-box to be related to Frog later on that evening.

"D'you mean to say," he asked in an astonished voice, "that you actually ran in the Derby?"

"Oh, yes," said Horse casually, as if running in the Derby was quite an ordinary everyday event. "Could have won it too . . . if I'd wanted to," he added as an afterthought.

"D'you mean to say," said Timmy, "that you didn't *try?*" Memories of all the shillings he'd put on horses which had gone monotonously floating down the drain (the shillings, *not* the horses) in his old London days, came painfully back to him and he sounded really shocked—as indeed he was.

"No," said Horse, "I didn't."

"But why?" stammered the incredulous Tortoise.

"Well, to tell you the truth," answered Horse, "I just couldn't be bothered." And he yawned again, although this time he did attempt to cover it up by lifting one hoof slightly and gazing at Timmy from behind it, with great big sorrowful eyes. He was a very well-bred horse and he had no wish to appear rude. It was just that he was terribly, terribly tired of it all.

"Oh," said Timmy. "B-but wasn't that very naughty of you? I—I—I mean to say, aren't you supposed to always try your hardest in a race?"

"Yes, I suppose so," answered Horse. "Some of them do, but really I don't see the use of it. Actually," he added, "I won quite a few races when I was a two-year-old, but what did I get out of it? Nothing. . . . Exactly. . . . Precisely. . . . Positively. . . . NOTHING. . . ."

"B-b-but the Honor and Glory," stammered Timmy. "The Pride . . ."

"Honor and Glory! Fiddlesticks," retorted the racehorse. "You can't eat *those* things. Owners get money and cups and what-have-you. Trainers and jockeys get money and what do *I* get? A pat on the neck, a mouthful of grass (if I'm lucky) and then back to the same old business *all* over again. No," he added sleepily, "it really isn't worth it. Although

it's dull here in this field and Farmer Crossbones
is a heavy old body to carry about, it's a much pleas-
anter life, believe me, and I'm not ambitious. Another thing too, little friend, which I haven't told
you." And here a glimmer of disgust flickered into
his languid eyes. "They insulted me."

"Oh, no, did they really?" said Timmy, his right
ear, which was the most inquisitive one, flapping
wildly.

"Yes, they did." And Horse's voice sank to a
whisper and, holding his hoof to his mouth, he
breathed down the most inquisitive ear. "They
called me a Dog!"

"Oh, no," said Timmy, thoroughly shocked.
"How could they call you a Dog when you're a
Horse?"

Horse threw back his head and laughed and
laughed and laughed until Timmy began to think
he'd been taken ill or something.

"Haw . . . haw . . . haw . . . haw," he laughed.
"You really are a nice, funny little tortoise. Dog,"
he explained patiently at last, when he had finished
laughing, "is 'racing language' for a horse that
won't try."

"Then you *are* a Dog?" said Timmy in a sort of
hushed voice. "There's no getting round it, is there?"

"Oh, dear," sighed Horse. "So *you* think so too, do you? And just as we were getting on so well," he added regretfully.

"Wouldn't you try if you had something to race *for?*" asked Timmy. "Loads of nice juicy carrots or something?"

"H-m-mm-m," mused Horse. "That depends. I might and on the other hand," he added, "I might not. Depends on who I was working for. *That,* little Tortoise, is a very important point. I certainly wouldn't if I still had to run races for that horrible Toad."

"Toad?" asked Timmy in astonishment. "What Toad?"

"Samuel Goad I believe his name was. A horrible fellow. Dreadfully bad mannered."

"Oh," breathed Timmy in a scarcely audible whisper. "That explains everything. Fancy having to belong to a man like that! No wonder you didn't like it."

He was so pleased that now, in his eyes, the character of his new-found friend had been completely whitewashed all over.

"Would you—w-w-would you," he stammered, "er—I mean, supposing y-you were to work for somebody you like—er—w-would you—?"

"You mean, supposing I were to belong to somebody nice, like you, for instance, my nice little friend, would I run my hardest?"

"Y-y-yes," answered Timmy hopefully. "Th-that's just what I mean."

"You bet I would," answered Horse gravely. "You bet I would." And looking up from his munching he gave the most enormous wink which made him (Timmy) his slave for life.

"P-p-please, Horse," begged Timothy, "tell me your name. I m-must get back. It's getting late and I *do* want to tell my friend Frog *all* about you. Racehorses all have names and he just won't belive you're a REAL racehorse if you haven't got a REAL name."

Horse sighed—a long, deep, weary sigh. "Well, if you *must* know," he said, "come closer and I will tell you." And he breathed heavily into Timmy's ear. "Promise you won't laugh?"

"I promise," said Timmy, and he clasped Horse's large hoof in his (at least the tip of it, because he couldn't get hold of it all) just to show him how much he really meant it.

"It's MARMADUKE," whispered Horse. "Isn't it awful?" And his face went the color of a ripe tomato from his nose to his ears.

"Marmaduke," murmured Timothy rapturously. "I think it's a *beautiful* name!"

"Oh, you don't! Do you really, dear kind little Tortoise?" cried the owner of it, happily, hardly daring to believe his ears.

"Yes, I do," replied Timmy firmly. "And what's more," he added, struck suddenly by the most wonderful, the most strange, the most incredible SOMETHING which resolved itself into an IDEA inside

"I think it's a beautiful name!"

him, whirling round like a huge gaily colored balloon in front of his very eyes. "And what's more," he repeated, hardly believing that it was *he,* Timothy Tortoise, who was saying these words, "one day it's going to be a GREAT and FAMOUS name, and all other racehorses will remember it for years and years and years!"

So that was how the whole thing started—"TIMOTHY TORTOISE's FAMOUS PLAN."

But that looks like the heading of another chapter. And, anyway, this one has gone on long enough already. It's late and Timmy must return to Frogmorton with the milk; Marmaduke must lie down in the sweet meadow grass and dream; it's long past my bedtime and in any case, my pen has run out of ink.

CHAPTER TEN

Conversation With Aunt Sophie

AT DINNER that evening, Timmy forgot all about his aching limbs and his tired old heart. He was all aglow, fired with a tremendous enthusiasm which even the logical, commonsensical frog could do nothing to abate.

"Don't you *see*, Froggy," he persisted, "it's a chance in a million. There he is at the bottom of the park. A beautiful, shiny, ready-made RACEHORSE. Ready to run for his life for you! MARMADUKE," he murmured. "What a beautiful name!"

"Hrmm," grunted Frog. "I know more about racehorses than you do. My grandfather owned 'em. Dozens of 'em. Nearly broke 'im. Unreliable, unpredictable creatures he called 'em—*and* he was right. You leave 'im where he is. We've got enough trouble on our hands already without goin' gamblin' on racehorses."

"B-b-but this wouldn't be gambling," argued Timmy. "I have his word for it. He would run his very *hardest* for you and, after all, if he could have won the Derby, he should be able to win any ordinary sort of race quite easily—on his head, in fact," he added in a professional sort of way.

"Horses don't run on their heads," put in Frog grumpily. "Anyhow, racehorses have to be trained. You can't just go and buy one one minute and run it the next. It's not as simple as all that."

"Oh, I know, I know," answered Timmy, "but couldn't we find a trainer for him? Oh, *please,* Froggy. Think what it would mean. Money to pay all your taxes with! Perhaps," he muttered wistfully, "we could even buy a new lawn mower." And added almost under his breath, "a motor one."

"Great heavens!" laughed the practical Frog. "You'll be havin' us with a new motor car like Goad's next. The horse has got to win first, y'know."

Mention of the name "Goad" brought a last desperate gleam into Timmy's eye. It was a trump card and he played it.

"Just think, Froggy. What fun it would be to win a race with Goad's own horse that he'd sold to old Father Crossbones for a mere fifteen pounds."

"Hrmmm," mused Frog, hesitating in the middle

of a mouthful of soup. He seemed to be poised on the edge of a decision and like a diver he waited, hovering on the brink, uncertain whether to take the plunge. Suddenly he brought his spoon down on his plate with a bang.

"Dash it, Timmy! I believe you've got something there. After all, when you come to think of it, what have we got to lose? And can't you just see his face? Ha—ha—ha—ha," he chuckled, shaking his sides with laughter. Then as if by the jerk of a rope his laughing stopped and he returned wearily to his soup.

"Better forget it, old boy. I'd forgotten that we haven't anything to buy this remarkable animal with, let alone to risk on his possible victory."

But Timmy having got so far, was quite determined not to lose an inch of ground.

"What about that picture of your Great Aunt Sophie? The one you always said looked like a green currant bun? Remember? Isn't it supposed to be by Sir Joshua someone or other? Couldn't you sell that?"

"What," cried the scandalized Frog, whose ancestors, even if they were currant buns, were still his ancestors. "Sell Aunt Sophie to buy a RACE-HORSE!"

Put like that it did sound rather a drastic thing to do, even to the madly enthusiastic Timmy.

"Anyhow, I am not sure she is by Sir Joshua. If she is, of course, I've really no right to sell her. She's an 'heirloom' and should stay in the family."

"Let's go and ask her," said Timmy, who was by now sunk, hook, line, and sinker in this adventure, and for him there was no turning back.

So they stood in the hall, in the dim light of the tall mullioned windows. The first stars were appearing in the early spring night and Frog had to bring a candle to enable the two of them to see the face of the famous old Lady Sophia, staring down with big black boot-button eyes on all that went on beneath.

"Well, Aunt Sophie, my dear," said Frog, "here's the whole position." And he related in his clear, bold Fitzherbert voice all that had happened. Without elaborating one single detail, he described quite calmly the awful predicament that he was in.

"So there you are, you see," he ended, looking up. "Or rather," he added, "there *we* are. What do you think we ought to do about it?"

The two animals waited in silence for her answer. Would she speak? Or was she just paint and canvas, hopelessly encased in the past?

The grandfather clock ticked on. The moments

passed and still that stout figure in the gold-carved frame stared down at them, grim and immovable.

"It's no good, Froggy," said Timmy sadly. "She's just a picture, poor old thing. Still, there was no harm in trying." And they both turned away. Two sad, disconsolate little figures in the semi-darkness.

But as they turned, a flicker from the candle shed an extra gleam of light straight into the face of Great Aunt Sophie, and in that single flicker Frog suddenly saw something which made his heart miss a beat. Yes. He could swear it. The old lady gave him the most obvious and premeditated WINK.

It was so surprising in an old lady of her age and stately demeanor, that Frog nearly fell over backwards. It made her look positively rakish.

"H-m-m," she said, clearing her throat. "So you're in tr-r-rrouble, Fitzherbert, eh?" The voice boomed to the very rafters of the great hall and echoed like thunder through the passages. It was dreadfully alarming. Timmy would have run like a rabbit if only his feet hadn't been, somehow, cemented into the floor. He was unable to move and stood rooted to the spot, every nerve in his body jangling like a million church bells at a wedding. If only he hadn't suggested this ridiculous idea. He wanted to ask Froggy to run away with him. Back into the

"So you're in tr-r-rrrouble, Fitzherbert, eh?"

safety of the dining-room. Out into the sweet-scented night. Anywhere. Only to get away from this spooky voice from the past.

But Frog stood his ground. After all, they had started this thing. They must go on with it.

"So you're going to sell Frogmorton, eh?" boomed the voice.

"We're going to have to," answered Frog as steadily as he could.

"Otherwise, you were thinking of selling *me?* Is that it?" went on Aunt Sophie relentlessly.

"Yes," murmured Frog.

"H-m-m," grunted Aunt Sophie. "I'm not worth as much as you think. That lazy painter-feller handed me on to one of his pupils to do. 'Gettin' too old for 'is job,' I said. Still, I suppose I'm worth about five hundred pounds. Would that be enough to purchase this good-fer-nothin' racehorse you're after?"

"Oh, yes," broke in Timmy excitedly. "M-m-more than enough."

"Tell your friend to keep his mouth shut and speak when he's spoken to," ordered Aunt Sophie, in her most commanding voice. "We haven't even been introduced yet. . . . H-her—hmmm."

Timmy wished the floor would open and swallow him up.

"Well," went on the formidable old lady, "I'm quite prepared to be sold if it's going to be any help. Always did rather like a bit of a gamble meself. As I always said to your old Great Great Uncle Fitzherbert, 'Nothin' venture, nothin' win.' One thing, however, I do insist upon, and that is that I shall be sold at Christie's, in London. It's the *best* place. I wouldn't dream of goin' anywhere else. Good-bye, Fitzherbert."

And with that the little dumpy figure seemed to recede into her frame and retreat back into the past, and the boot-button eyes once more stared down out of the round greenish bun-like face. The hands no longer fingered the half-open fan, but lay placidly folded together in her lap and Aunt Sophie was just a picture on the wall once more.

Timmy and Frog hurried back into the dining-room and silently finished off a whole bottle of port before they could, either of them, trust their own voices.

Then, "Well!" said Frog, "I never guessed Aunt Sophie had it in 'er. She's quite a sporting old girl. I'm sorry I ever called her a currant bun. Here's to 'er," he added, draining his glass.

"Whoopee," shouted Timmy, and they both sat back and laughed till the tears ran into their boots.

CHAPTER ELEVEN

Training Marmaduke

Stranger, have you ever been
Up on the downs in the morning dew?
Where the sunlight lies on the golden turf
Which remembers days which no man knew?
When the air is so still and quiet and sweet
And the swallows dive suddenly under your feet
And the larks sing high and the plovers call
And swiftly, swiftly, best of all,
Like gorgeous ghosts, the horses pass
A wave of shadows on the grass.

So THAT was how it came about that Frog became the owner of Marmaduke, the retired racehorse.

Aunt Sophie actually fetched seven hundred guineas at the sale. Thirty pounds went on buying Marmaduke and one hundred and fifty pounds was put by, by the prudent Frog, for training expenses and entrance fees for the races.

"That leaves about five hundred pounds to bet on him when the time comes," said Frog.

"Good heavens!" cried Timmy. "You're not going to put the whole lot on at once, are you?"

"Why not?" said Frog. "It's no good doin' these things by halves, yer know. May as well 'be hanged for a sheep as a lamb,' so they say. If 'e don't win the first time, we can't afford to go on feeding 'im, so we might as well have a proper bash, win or lose."

It was the old Fitzherbert Frog speaking in the old Fitzherbert manner, but to Timmy, who was always inclined to begin things with great gusto and then get very cold feet in the middle, it was, to say the least of it, rather flabbergasting. Five hundred pounds on a horse! And there was Frog talking about it as though he were buying bull's-eyes at the village post office. Timmy shook in his shoes, but his eyes looked with mute admiration at his friend. What a wonderful fellow he was! Oh, brave, fearless Frog! "If only I could be like that," thought Timmy, and sighed, knowing that however hard he tried, he never would be.

It was now the middle of May. Frog had discovered an old Irish steeplechase jockey called Murphy

Maguire, to whom he entrusted the training of Marmaduke. He was a tiny little bent-up fellow with a face like a pickled walnut and a broad Irish voice that came out of his boots.

"Ach . . . yer honner, but it t'is a ghreaate horrse ye have here," he would say. "A graaate horrse—an' no mistake."

And early every morning, before the village was awake, the two of them, Murphy on top and Marmaduke underneath, would clip-clop quietly through the park gates and up the hill onto the downs for their morning exercise.

Every now and then Timothy Tortoise and Frog would set the alarm clock and, plunging their heads into a basin of cold water to clear the sleep from their eyes, would take old Rolly (the Rolls) out of *his* stable and puff and pant up to the top of the hill to watch the "work," as Frog rather grandly called it. He was already getting to be a keen racehorse owner and sometimes, when Rolly coughed and spat and wouldn't start, he was apt to say angry words to him and hit him with the starting handle (which wasn't really fair, because Rolly was an old gentleman unaccustomed to getting up so early).

One morning, on one of these expeditions, Maguire rode up to the two animals, who were stand-

ing behind a gorse bush with their binoculars handy
on the ground beside them.

"Tell me, Mr. Frog," he said, "how many miles
an hour would that moty car of yours be affter goin'
if you was ter dhrive it as fast as it would go?"

"I've never done such a thing," answered Frog
huffily.

"Well, will you do it now, jest to please Marmaduke here? Ye see, yer honner, the poor fellow has
no friend to gallop *with* and so we have no *now*tion
how fast he can go. Now, if you was to dhrive that
vehicle of yours along by the side of us, we could
see how fast we was goin'—and that would please
him, and *you* would be the wiser fer knowin', now
wouldn't yer?"

Timmy was delighted with the idea and was all
for putting it into operation straight away, but
Frog had strong misgivings. In spite of hitting him
occasionally with the starting handle, he was really
very fond of Rolly. He had been a good friend
for nearly thirty years, and to have to use him now
as a sort of trial horse for Marmaduke seemed a
little hard on the old thing and rather beneath his
dignity.

However, in the end, when Maguire pointed out
to him that some sort of a trial was rather a neces-

sary part of Marmaduke's preparation, expediency got the better of caution and Frog agreed to allow Rolly to "run."

Maguire was to bring Marmaduke up the gradual incline to the top of the hill where he was to be joined by Frog and Timmy in Rolly, and they were to race the remaining mile and a quarter neck and neck.

That was the IDEA. What actually happened was slightly different.

All went well until they had gone about a mile, bumping and crashing over the mossy turf, sometimes up and sometimes down. Several times they hit their heads the most terrible crack on the roof, and then down they would come wallop! on the ancient creaking springs, only to be thrown sky-high again as they struck the next hillock.

"Oh. . . . AH. . . . OOH. . . . GRACIOUS," gulped Timmy, trying to get his breath.

But Frog drove like a demon with his foot flat down on the accelerator.

"Look, Timmy," he shouted, "the speedometer! Forty miles an hour!"

And still Marmaduke gained on them. He seemed to be having a private race with the wind. The pace was terrific. Frog bent over the wheel, perspiration pouring down his face. "Go on, go on," he shouted, but whether he was really shouting at the car or at Marmaduke was a debatable point.

He seemed to be having a private race with the wind

Then, just as it looked as though old Rolly was going to make up a bit of ground coming round the turn, there was a deafening roar from somewhere deep inside his iron stomach and with a great enormous BANG! he burst. His radiator blew off and bits of metal flew in all directions. Then he gave a gigantic sigh and settled himself down, the rest of his body seemed to disappear between his four wheels, and the two animals found themselves sitting on the ground.

"That's done it," said Frog. "Poor old Rolly. It was that last bit that killed him."

"Is he dead?" asked Timmy querulously.

"Oh, no," said Frog. "I dare say he'll mend, but it will take weeks and meantime we'll have nothing to go to Ascot in."

"Ascot?" ventured Timmy. The word seemed almost too grand and splendid to pronounce.

"Yes, Ascot, my boy," shouted Frog, banging him on the back with a tremendous thump. "I discovered last night that this horse of ours is still entered in the Gold Cup. That idiot Goad must've forgotten to take 'im out of it before he sold 'im, and 'e sold 'im with *all* his engagements, so 'e's still able to run in it—and what's more, he'll win it, Timmy, my old pal, he'll *WIN* it."

Timmy had never seen his friend so excited before. The fact that his only car lay in little bits all round him seemed to have passed him by and he sat with his eyes glistening, gazing towards the horizon, where the flying Marmaduke could just be seen disappearing over the skyline.

"Forty miles an hour at the end of a mile and a half," he murmured. "The Gold Cup is ours!"

CHAPTER TWELVE

The Great Day

THE GREAT DAY dawned bright and clear. Murphy Maguire took Marmaduke up on the downs for what he called a short "pipe-opener," then he was put into Farmer Crossbones's best cattle truck and driven by his son William in state to Ascot Racecourse. (The Crossbones family were just as excited over the whole business as Frog himself.)

Timothy, of course, got himself into the most hopeless tangle with his tail coat and smart pin-stripe trousers, which he had hired for the occasion from a famous firm in London. Somehow or other the beautiful lavender-colored waistcoat, which had looked so splendid on the tailor's dummy in the catalogue, looked like a dish rag on Timmy when he put it on, riding up under his chin, so that it

was more like a ruff than a waistcoat. He pulled
and tugged at the coat to make it meet over his
middle and so hide the disgraceful thing but, try as
he would, it wouldn't. In the end Frog came to the
rescue and looped an enormous gold watch chain
from one side to the other and if the result wasn't
exactly neat, it was, to say the least of it, impres-
sive.

"You look like the Mayor and Corporation," said
Frog.

"Do I?" beamed Timmy, delighted that he looked
like *something* at any rate, and not like a rather
harassed tortoise in borrowed clothes which didn't
fit him.

Frog, of course, looked MAGNIFICENT. He smelt
powerfully of moth balls and if you looked closely,
his shining top hat, which was the one he used to
wear for hunting and had belonged to two generations of Frogs, bore traces of some of the thick fences
it had been through in the past. But the whole effect,
viewed from a distance, was very elegant.

They had to start very early to catch the first
train from Coppertown. Grubbins was driving them
to the station in the milk float with Harry the Hunter
already harnessed and waiting at the front door.

"Come on, Timmy," shouted Frog as, regardless

of his Ascot finery, he slid down the banisters. "Don't bother with yer old hat, it looks splendid. Better take a mackintosh and galoshes. Never can tell

Dressing for Ascot

about the weather. Here are yer race glasses," he added, as he handed him an old pair of his own. And with a wave of his beautifully rolled umbrella to Matt, who stood in the hall, wagging his tail, they were suddenly seated behind Harry the Hunter.

Frog had tucked a small travelling rug round Timmy and before you could say, "Jack Robinson" they were off, Frog driving, of course, and old Grubbins sitting respectfully in the front with the milk cans.

They bowled merrily along the country lanes in the bright morning sunshine and the birds whistled and sang in the hedgerows and chirruped, "Good luck, Mr. Frog," as they went by. The bees hummed and the butterflies flitted to and fro. Everything and everyone seemed as busy as could be. Young Willy Jones on his tractor touched his cap, and shouted, "Good luck, Mr. Frog," although nobody could hear him above the noise of the tractor.

A magpie flew out of the hedge and made Harry the Hunter jump to one side. "Good luck, Mr. Frog," it squawked.

"That's put the lid on it," said Frog in a gruff voice. "Never have any luck when I see a magpie."

"Quick, look! There's another one flying after him," shouted Timmy. "*That's* all right, Froggy. Two for joy, you know."

"Of course there's nothing in it *really,*" went on Frog in his usual matter-of-fact voice, just as if he hadn't heard. "Don't believe in any of these superstitions really. Lot of nonsense the whole thing—walkin' under ladders and everything. Stupid," he added after a pause. "Just plain *stupid*."

But he didn't admit even to himself that he was quite glad, all the same, that he'd seen the other magpie just in time.

At last they got to the station. At least it seemed "at last" to Timmy who was all nerved up in a tight hard ball inside. He had to keep one hand firmly pressed on his tummy to stop it from careering madly round in circles as though it had a whole regiment of mice chasing it. Frog looked so calm and collected. You might have thought he was going to a Church Council Meeting instead of to Ascot to see his horse run for the Gold Cup and for the whole of Frogmorton into the bargain.

"Good morning, sir," said the Stationmaster, as he helped Frog out of the milk float. "Lovely morning. Looks like keeping fine too. I wish you the best of luck, sir."

"Thank you, Alfred," said Frog. "I expect we shall need it," he added.

Timmy wondered whether there were mice chasing his stomach too. It didn't look as though there were. But then, of course, Frog had such SELF-CONTROL. You never could tell with Frog.

Fifteen minutes' wait and then, away up the hill, they suddenly caught sight of a puff of smoke.

"She's dead on time," said Alfred with a satisfied note in his voice.

(Dead on time meant that "she" was only ten minutes late instead of twenty.) No doubt "she" was realizing the importance of the occasion.

Once settled into their seats in an empty first-class compartment, the time seemed to drag by with lead in its boots.

To Timmy, who was unused to travelling anyway, it was the longest journey he had ever experienced. (Except, perhaps, the one, so long ago, when he had first come down to Frogmorton.)

"Oh, dear, Froggy," he sighed. "Will we *ever* get there?"

" 'Course we will," said Frog. "Don't fuss. Here! Let's have a go at those sandwiches, shall we?" And both pulled fat packages out of their mackintosh pockets and started chewing to pass the time.

They had to change twice on the journey, but at last they arrived at Ascot Station and it seemed to Timmy as if all the world and his wife were there. What a crowd! And what finery! Men in top hats and morning-coats, ladies in silk dresses and fur wraps and huge hats like bunches of Shirley poppies in full bloom. Timmy had never seen anything like it. He gaped and gaped and gaped.

"Come *on,*" said Frog impatiently, seizing him by the paw. "Look! Now we have missed that taxi. We'll have to walk."

And so walk they did. All the way up the road to Ascot Heath, arriving in the paddock very out of breath, just as the first race was being run.

Muttering something about having to go and find a jockey, Frog disappeared into the milling crowd and Timmy was left to potter about on his own and stare and stare and stare.

What an astonishing sight it was! All these beautifully dressed people wandering about on the emerald-green grass as if they lived there. Nobody noticed a little old wrinkle-faced tortoise who stood with his nose pressed to the rails quite dumbfounded by the whole proceedings.

At last it was time for the big race of the day. THE GOLD CUP. Frog had already been up to the very top end of the paddock to help Maguire put the saddle on Marmaduke, and had returned to find Timmy, still standing by the rails which led into the Royal Enclosure, just in time to drag him, rather unwillingly, into the center of the parade ring. "Oh, please leave me here, Froggy," he said.

"Don't talk nonsense, old chap," said Frog impatiently. "After all, this whole thing was *your* idea to start with and you're jolly well going to help me see it through."

"Oh, dear," sighed Timmy. "I don't think I'll ever be able to stand it. All those people staring at me and my coat doesn't fit or anything! I th-th-think I'm going to be sick," he added desperately.

"No, you're not," said Frog firmly, and once again took him manfully by the paw and led him right into the center of the ring, where all the famous owners and trainers and jockeys were standing, just as if he did this sort of thing every day of his life.

" 'Mornin', Frog," said one distinguished-looking gentleman with a curling grey moustache and a beautiful dark-red carnation in his buttonhole.

" 'Mornin', Percy," returned Frog nonchalantly, although it was the middle of the afternoon.

Timmy gaped. He had seen this man's photograph in the morning paper only the day before and he was none other than the Senior Steward of the Jockey Club. How simply *flabbergasting* it all was! But how WONDERFULLY EXCITING! And there, coming towards them was a little man with beetling eyebrows and an unmistakable walk.

" 'Mornin', Frog," said one distinguished-looking gentleman

" 'Mornin', sir," said this gentleman, smiling as he went by.

" 'Mornin', Gordon," answered Frog. None other than Sir Gordon Richards himself!

"Good gracious!" murmured Timmy to himself.
"What will happen next?" And his heart turned a
double somersault and luckily landed the right side
up as Frog put a nice warm comforting paw in his,
and said:

"Cheer up, old boy. It'll soon be over and then you
can go back to your precious old garden!"

"Oh, dear, *dear* Froggy," thought Timmy. "How
like him to think of me at this of all times. What a
dear, kind, wonderful animal he is." And with a
great effort of will, he commanded his wavering
stomach, which had threatened to rise up in revolt
only a few moments before, to lie down and remain
in its proper place.

So there they were. And now in front of them,
almost as though he'd been spirited up from the
underworld, for Timmy at least had never noticed
him arrive, stood a small, powerfully built little
man with hunched-up shoulders and eyes that
seemed to swizzle in all directions at once, whose
name was COSTER LOTT and into whose hands had
been entrusted the safe steering of Marmaduke.

Timmy didn't like the look of him at all, but it
seemed that he was the only jockey they could get
and it was now too late to do anything about it.

And there was Marmaduke, looking like a prince,

strolling around the paddock as if he owned the whole racecourse and everyone on it.

People couldn't help noticing him. "Who is that beautiful chestnut?" they inquired, glancing at their cards on which they read:

13. Marmaduke 9 st. 0 lbs. *Trainer:* M. Maguire
    ch. c. by Marmalade—Greedy Duchess
    Mr. F. Fitzherbert Frog

"Oh!" they said. *"That* old dog. Fancy running *him* in the Gold Cup." And turned to look at something else.

Timmy hoped to goodness that poor Marmaduke hadn't heard. He felt that such a remark would have hurt him dreadfully.

As a matter of fact Marmaduke *did* hear, but instead of taking it to heart, he just lifted a hind leg and kicked the lady's hat off. "That'll teach her," he murmured—and it *did*.

At last it was time for the jockeys to get mounted. Maguire had a last word with Coster Lott.

"Arl ye hav' ter do, my lad, is ter stay in yer seat. The harsse will do the rest." And as if in confirmation of this statement, Marmaduke gave Timmy the most almighty wink, which was all the encouragement he needed to put his last ten shilling note on

the Totalizator (which in case you didn't know, is a
sort of thing like a giant threshing machine, only it
eats money instead of corn).

Frog had already invested all his five hundred
pounds with a well-known firm of bookmakers in
London called JOE ROOK LTD. at odds of 100-1.
"That'll make 'em sit up and think," chuckled Frog.
"Make that old Goad sit up a bit too." And a broad
grin of anticipation spread right across his face like
the rays of the rising sun. "I should just love to see
his face when he hears about it."

As a matter of fact, at this very moment Samuel
Goad and his little fat wife were seated in front
of the very latest design in television sets, watching
everything that was going on from the comfort of
two large armchairs.

"Look, Sam," said his wife in a little fat squeaky
voice, "there's that silly old idiot Frog and his stupid
little tortoise friend. What on earth can they be doing at Ascot? *And* in the Royal Enclosure too!"

"I've no idea, dear," answered her husband,
lighting another large cigar and settling himself
back in his seat to watch the parade for the big
race.

CHAPTER THIRTEEN

The Race

MARMADUKE hated racing. But now, somehow, it was different. He had two friends who believed in him. One indeed, albeit only a tortoise, who thought he was MARVELLOUS. *And they trusted him.* That was the thing that mattered. Well, he wouldn't disappoint them. He'd show the world that Marmaduke was a name to be reckoned with in racing.

Oh! It was fun to be on Ascot Heath again, feeling the emerald green springy turf under his feet, and the packed crowds waiting in the stands to cheer him home. He gave a great bound and kicked his hind legs in the air, as he cantered down to the post, all but unseating the unfortunate Coster, who bumped his nose on one of the plaits in Marmaduke's mane and swore a very unprintable swear in the best Lott tradition.

" 'Ere steady on, clumsy," he shouted as soon as he regained his lost "pedal." "We'd better stay together afore the race has started, any'ow. Lord knows what'll happen afterwards," he muttered under his breath, remembering some of the tales he'd heard from other jockeys of his mount's past history. " 'Spect we shall be joining in the Royal Percession when they start racing again to-morrow. Still, a fiver's a fiver and a ride's a ride," he consoled himself as they approached the starting-gate. " 'Ere goes," he stammered gallantly, as a few moments later the tapes went up and he found himself lolloping along quite happily in the rear of the field, about ten lengths behind the last horse.

Marmaduke seemed to be in no kind of hurry at all. In fact, to the casual observer, it looked as though he had already lost all interest in the proceedings and was just following the others round for the good of his health.

When they'd covered nearly a mile of the course and were passing the stands the first time round, Timmy Tortoise could hardly bear to look, Marmaduke was *so* far behind. It looked as if he were having a private race all on his own, but Frog kept his

*The tapes went up and he found himself lolloping along
quite happily in the rear of the field*

glasses firmly glued to his eyes and whatever he was
thinking to himself ("Stupid old fool! Ought to have
known better—trusting a good-fer-nothin' racehorse at *my* age!") he never transmitted any of his
thoughts or fears to his neighbors. (As you have no
doubt noticed by now, FROG WAS A VERY BRAVE AND
NOBLE ANIMAL.)

Some of the people standing by the rails laughed
and cheered as Marmaduke went by. "Go it, HAND-
SOME," they shouted. "Why not wait for 'em till

next time round?" And others in the stands murmured, "There he goes, the old dog. Up to his old tricks again. Not trying a yard."

(Goad, watching his television, had still no idea that Marmaduke was in the race at all, as the television camera didn't bother to stretch itself that far back.)

Still the leaders forged ahead and still the bright chestnut, bearing the famous ancient green and gold colors of the Fitzherbert Frogs, seemed content to lollop along in the rear with the utmost unconcern. "Who cares?" he seemed to be saying to himself, and it really seemed as though nobody *did*. Nobody, that is, except Frog, and poor Timmy Tortoise (who had hidden his face in his hands and daren't even peep through his fingers), and the Crossbones family biting their nails in the Grand Stand, and Maguire beginning to curse just a little bit in Irish.

"Strike me pink," thought Coster to himself, "I'll be still runnin' at Christmas at this rate." But just as the thought reached his brain from his boots (a distance of only about forty inches) something happened which made him sit down in his saddle and take notice. Marmaduke WOKE UP. (Actually, he'd never really been asleep. He was just waiting, letting all the other horses get nice and tired.)

As they passed Swinley Bottom he began to move forward towards the last horse, who was now twenty lengths in front of him. Imperceptibly at first, and then gradually faster and faster until it seemed to Coster, on top, that the two of them were flying, not touching the ground at all.

One by one, Marmaduke overhauled the other horses. First The Custard King, then Admiral's All, then High Life and Bonnie Prince Charlie, lying close together, then Careless II and Passing Fancy, then Shady Jane and Kitty-Wink, until he was lying just behind the leaders, Spanish Onion and Strike-a-Light. The latter was still going well, but Spanish Onion was beginning to feel the pace. Marmaduke knew that he could pass him any time he wanted to, but like the old campaigner he was, he waited, not attempting to go to the front too soon.

This sudden arrival on the scene of old "dog" Marmaduke, the unconsidered "outsider," had caused a hubbub on the stands and the bookmakers were in a fever of excitement. "Two to one Marmaduke," they shouted, but everybody was too busy watching the contest to pay much attention.

"He's shot his bolt now," said one of the knowledgeable ones, who felt that such a thing *couldn't* happen even in the most unpredictable sport of all. "Look! Strike-a-Light's still a long way in front! Strike-a-Light will win!" (Strike-a-Light was, of course, the favorite.)

But Frog said nothing. Perhaps his breath came a little faster—only because he had unconsciously been holding it for two minutes, but he said nothing. Timmy, on the other hand, was jumping up and down like a Jack-in-the-box and yelling for all he was worth.

"Come *on,* Marmaduke. Come on, old boy! Oh, come on! Oh! Oh! Oh!" Until he was absolutely hoarse and the people all round him thought he had gone a bit dotty.

Frog seemed quite oblivious to everything. He just waited and hoped and prayed and said nothing.

Then just as they rounded the final bend into the straight and the bell rang, Marmaduke felt that his moment had come. He swept past Spanish Onion as though he wasn't there and now he was level with Strike-a-Light's tail. Now with only about three hundred yards to go, he was level with Strike-a-Light's girth.

"Come on, Marmaduke!"

"I'll show you, you young Jackanapes, Derby winner or not," he whispered, gritting his teeth, and with an imperial sweep of his tail, he swept past the big raking bay and went on to win by fifteen lengths, the easiest winner of the Gold Cup that there had been for many a long year.

The people gasped and then, as Marmaduke returned to walk sedately into the Winner's Enclosure, trying so hard to look unconcerned, with Coster, smiling all over his face until it looked as if it would split in two, they began to cheer. And they cheered and they cheered and they cheered until the stands rocked. An old forgotten-about racehorse had come back to racing and had beaten last year's Derby winner, and won the Gold Cup, and his owner was a frog and a much respected one at that, and it was a grand and unforgettable thing to have happened.

And there was Frog standing proudly by Marmaduke's head having his photograph taken.

(At this moment Goad threw a brass coal scuttle at the television set and broke it. He had to buy Mrs. Goad a new and even more expensive one, so it didn't do any good.)

And a few moments later, there was Frog hurrying along to the Royal Box, having been summoned by a distinguished-looking gentleman from the Royal Household to an interview with Her Majesty the Queen!

Timmy stood in a little place by himself, trying not to get in anybody's way and hoping that nobody would notice him, and tried to think. And all his thoughts were so amazing and wonderful, and they

Standing proudly by Marmaduke's head having his photograph taken

Goad threw a brass coal scuttle at the television set and broke it

all crowded in on top of one another so fast that he had to take off his top hat to give his brain some air (hoping that nobody would see). Then he sat down in a corner by the number board, and said quietly to himself, "Oh, my goodness!" And then, *"Well! Well!! Well!!!"*

So much had happened since that never-to-be-forgotten day when he had taken the train to Coppertown to stay at Frogmorton for Christmas. So many adventures to happen to an old partly-worn-out tortoise. Frogmorton was safe now, thanks to Marmaduke (and Aunt Sophie), and perhaps in a roundabout sort of way, thanks to himself (this thought made him blush and go pink round the ears, but it was rather a nice feeling all the same).

Now Frog would be able to go on living at Frog-morton as long as he lived and breathed and—oh, lovely, blissful thought!—he, Timmy, would be able to stay with him; anyhow, for another month, or perhaps two months. Anyway, he'd stay till the dahlias were out. Perhaps he might wait until the chrysanthemums came. Then there was Christmas! Another Christmas at Frogmorton! And then, the first snowdrops would lift their little lonely white heads through the cold earth. And then the prim-roses would come. And then the daffodils. The spring—the loveliest time of all. Well . . . per-haps! It was all a long time ahead. A lovely, long time to plan and to dream. . . .

So it was that, as I had hoped in the beginning, everyone (except Samuel Goad) was HAPPY EVER AFTER, which is just as it should be. And as Frog stood, hat in hand, talking to Her Majesty in the Royal Box—underneath the number board in the paddock, by a big iron wastepaper basket where people threw their old Totalizator tickets and ciga-rette ends, a funny little old tortoise lay curled up

fast asleep, dreaming of a garden in the springtime. . . .

Dreaming of a garden in the springtime